ATTORNEYS

AFTER THE CRASH

Tyler Coulson

THE WALKOUT SYNDICATE
CHICAGO

THE WALKOUT SYNDICATE LLC
CHICAGO, ILLINOIS

info@thewalkout.com

www.thewalkout.com

ISBN
978-0-9856119-5-8

Dedication

This little ditty is dedicated to Professor Longhair, for that one riff of his; to Justice John Paul Stevens, for that one riff of his; to a lady I know, for that one riff of hers; and to Mabel, who walked a very long way with me.

"First thing we do, let's kill all the lawyers."
-- Dick, in Shakespeare's 2 *Henry VI*, c. 1591

"First thing we do, let's preface every book about lawyers with that Shakespeare quote about killing lawyers. Context doesn't matter."
-- No One, Ever

"I could love you, but why begin it?
Cause there ain't any future in it.
Bye bye, Baby. Baby, goodbye."
--Frankie Vallie and the Four Seasons

ACT I: THE CRASH

The plane crashed without a sound. That surprised me, because I'd always imagined that a crash would be deafening—screaming children, bending steel, cracking bones, all of that. But the crash made no sound. I had fallen asleep with headphones on, so that's probably why I couldn't hear it. I woke up shortly before we hit and I looked over at Justine, two rows up and across the aisle; she looked back at me like she'd been checking to see when I would wake up and we smiled at each other. I started to say, "Justine, I...."

That's when the crash began.

No one screamed. Everyone held their breath and looked at one another until, without speaking, we all knew what was happening. The whole time I kept thinking, "Wow! Plane crashes sound just like the Bay City Rollers cover of *Bye Bye Baby* by the Four Seasons". Again, that was likely because I had left those headphones on. It was a hell of a crash and now I wish I'd been more awake through the whole thing so I could recount it better. But, then, who wants to have those kinds of memories?

I'm glad I was drunk.

A Boeing 737 holds 149 passengers plus crew; I looked that up. There were at least 140 of us on the plane, and probably a full flight, but I can't be sure because some people fell out of the plane and I never saw them again. Plus, I don't remember some of the details of the actual crash that well. I don't fly well and like to be pretty drunk before I get on a plane. I'd had several drinks before the flight in the airport bar with all the attorneys from my firm—not all, obviously, because the firm had like 2000 attorneys, but with quite a few of the attorneys in my group who were all on that flight with me. It takes a lot of drinks to get me on a plane and then after one or two on the plane I sleep. Usually.

This was all a long time ago. We lost track of time after the crash. It got ugly.

We hit nose first into the mountainside and right into a ravine or gully or canyon—let's call it a canyon. The canyon was narrow and the steep canyon sides ripped the wings off of the plane when we hit. That sent the plane spinning, so some people fell out of their seats. The twisting of the plane ripped the belly of it open and some people fell through the gap in the fuselage and I never saw them again and I thought "bye bye, Baby!" It looked very likely for a moment that the whole plane would split into two pieces and that we would *all* die. Justine was knocked out of her seat and she fell down through the gap in the floor of the plane, but a few attorneys from my practice group reached down and grabbed her as she fell. We pulled her up just before she was out of reach and then the plane twisted again and pulled the gap closed; a couple of people lost bits of their arms or legs when the plane pulled closed again. We smashed back and forth against the walls of the canyon, first to the right, then to the left, and then back and forth, and each time the impact was harder and more powerful than you can imagine. It must have been a spectacular thing to see from outside—not just spectacular like all airplane crashes are spectacular, but also because of the astronomical odds against how it happened. The odds against us crashing into that slender canyon were—I don't even know, but the mind boggles. We would have all died and been smashed to bits had we hit the mountain full against its face. But instead we approached it on a tangent, striking the side of it and glancing across the mountain before sliding into that canyon. I bet it was almost *beautiful* to watch, actually. From the outside, it probably looked like the pilots were skillful and determined, like they slid the plane into that slender canyon for a reason. Or maybe it looked like the plane wanted to wedge itself into the canyon because it was going home. Or maybe, if you go in for that kind of thing, like the hand of God came out of the sky, scooped up the plane, and deposited us into that canyon. Of course, it was the pilots who put us into the mountain, but still it's tempting to see the beauty in all things. Spectacular. From inside, though, it wasn't pleasant to see. It's probably a pretty awful thing to watch people die screaming, but I think it was worse to watch them die holding their breath. It wasn't just *fear*, is the thing—it was also knowledge, because they all knew they were dying. No one screamed. We all held our breath.

Then we hit a sharp bend or a crook in the canyon and, because the plane could not turn and was too long for the sharp bend, we slammed head first into the stone canyon wall. Our world inside the plane came to a stop in an instant. The seats broke free from the floor of the plane and we all went sliding forward into the seat backs in front of us; the rows of seats pushed together and the plane crumpled like an accordion's bellows. One little girl had her seat back tray table down when we hit and it nearly decapitated her. Almost everyone died. It was pretty much just we attorneys who lived. Not everyone died instantly, though. Once the plane came to a full stop there was a lot of groaning from the ones who'd been mortally injured but hadn't yet given up the ghost. My headphones fell off and were blaring, but tinny and distant, and I heard the groans of dying passengers intermittently over the buzzing earphones. And I thought, "Bye-bye, Baby."

Those of us who could walk or crawl left in a hurry through a big gash in the back of the plane near the tail where stone had ripped open a vertical hole in the shape of an eye. I was nearer the gash than most passengers so I was the first out, but those attorneys up at the front were clawing and screaming and climbing over corpses and broken plane bits. That sonofabitch Randall was the quickest to climb over all of the dead and the living—I'd never seen that strong and fat man move like that—and then he and I helped people step out of the gash and into the canyon where it was rather shaded but still brighter than in the dark inside the plane. We'd come to rest under a high canopy of pine trees and beneath a stone overhang. Once out of the

4

plane, you could stand and crane your neck and see back into the long dark tunnel of the plane's fuselage; it was a grim sight in there, so mostly people didn't look back. It was a tight squeeze to get all the living out of the back of the plane through the jagged gash, but we managed it and found that we were near a little patch of flat ground out there and a stream of clear water just a few hundred feet away at the base of the canyon, so it was a good place to recoup, to count our living, and to set about getting rescued. There was some chaos at first, but then everyone stopped shouting and then all you could hear were the attorneys arguing, the last groans of dying passengers, and, in the silent spaces between all that death, the gentle bubbling sound from the stream.

I should recount the names of the dead here, because I spent so much time writing them all down in a pocket notebook, but that's too morbid; I don't like to review the *Catalog of the Dead*. There were thirteen of us from the firm still living. We thirteen attorneys (as well as three other guys who lived through the crash) all stood around like idiots, absolutely in shock. I don't know how long it was before anyone spoke. It probably was not a long time, but it felt like a long time.

We were all in shock—genuine shock, I think—but shortly after the crash that sonofabitch Randall—the most senior attorney in my group—that sonofabitch Randall pulled aside the three other partners from the group who had lived through the crash and they all met in the shadow of the tree line to talk and to strategize about what we should do. One of the partners, Kent Elwes, was in pretty bad shape and the other partners had to carry him over to the meeting because he couldn't walk. Randall marched back over to our little camp when their meeting was over and he made the announcements. They put us into three groups—well, four groups if you count me. I can only imagine how much debate went into the formation of the groups as the partners argued back and forth about the relative importance of each group, the strengths and weaknesses of each of us attorneys stranded out there. The groups were as follows:

FIRE TEAM—PARTNER: RANDALL
Adam Billings: fifth year; injured, but not badly.
Jeffrey: fourth year; injured, emotionally distraught.
Lance Givens: first year; badly injured.

RESCUE TEAM—PARTNER: CARLA
Amy: eighth year, almost partner; bruises all over her body and almost certainly a broken shoulder.
George Barnes: sixth year; bruised, broken hand.
Kwame Gephardt: fifth year; injured.

WATER TEAM—PARTNER: TONY MARTIN
Denny Simons: sixth or seventh year; appeared to be uninjured.
Justine Moore: fourth year; the only other person besides me uninjured.
Muhammed bin Muhammed: second year; broken ribs and cuts on his face.

Randall appointed one of the partners to oversee each group. Carla oversaw Rescue Team, Tony Martin oversaw Water Team, and Randall oversaw Fire Team. That left me and Kent Elwes, and it was pretty clear that Kent was on his way out. Wait...that's fourteen? Maybe there were fourteen of us; there must have been. That's good, because thirteen is such an unlucky number. They all formed up in their groups and started milling around the campsite planning how to achieve their tasks, or how to "forge positive value-added outcomes through multi-talent synergies". Something like that.

"What about me?" I asked.

"Let's get everyone started first and then I'll talk to you," Randall said. "We've actually got a special duty for you."

They formed their teams and made plans on how to go about everything while I struck up a conversation with the three other guys who'd lived through the crash. They were law students on their way home after a week of call-back interviews with a prestigious firm. It was a genuinely prestigious firm, too, right on par with ours, so those law students wouldn't stop talking about it. One of them had also interviewed with one of our satellite offices—we had offices all over the world; we were a pretty big player in several markets. Each of those students was awful proud. They seemed like nice guys, but they were pretty shaken up and freaked out by the fact that only lawyers and law students had survived the crash, but I tried to explain to them that *everything's* a fifty-fifty chance—either it happens, or it doesn't. Like a coin toss. So the chances of a plane crashing and only lawyers surviving are fifty-fifty. They didn't see the humor in any of it. They were crying. Once everyone organized and the Water

Team headed out in search of water, Randall came over to me to discuss my assignment.

"Neal," he said, and motioned for me to sit beside the plane. He crouched beside me. "We're in a rough situation here. Aren't we?"

"I think so."

"Everyone's shaken up."

"Yes," I agreed.

"But you're calm? You're staying strong?"

"I'm trying," I said. And I was. I was really very calm, all things considered. It was almost a feeling of relief to be stranded out there—relief from the monotony, relief from the day-to-day. I don't know. It would be an adventure! Looking back, it's difficult for me to believe how calm I was, and I'd bet that I got on everyone's nerves because I was so calm, almost detached.

"Listen, what we need, and this is really the most important thing we can do right now, both for ourselves and to honor those who fell earlier, is to keep track of everyone. I'd like you to put together a list."

"Wait..." I interrupted him. Randall hated it when I interrupted him like that. "You want me to catalog the dead?"

"Yes," he said. "It's best practice. If you wouldn't mind. We've got water and fire and rescue all nailed down. But what we really need is someone on point to keep track of those who have died. Names, ages, vital information."

"You want me to go in there?" I asked. I pointed at the gash in the plane, beyond which was just darkness and corpses. "In there? And find out the names of all those dead people and then write down those names?"

"Yes. That would be just a great help right now. We've got to get through this as a team, Neal. But you know that as well as anyone. You're a team player, Neal, aren't you? I can count on you to take point on this one?"

"In there?"

"If you don't mind," he said.

"I don't think this is a good idea," I said. "It seems like kind of a waste."

"We've got everything else nailed down, Neal. But we really need you on this one. Can you do it?"

"Well of course I *can*," I said.

"I am thrilled that you understand how important this is, Neal. You're really doing me a favor on this one. I don't think...listen, this is just between you and me, but I don't think any of the others have the stomach to do it."

"In there?" I asked again. He smiled, told me I was a vital part of the team.

"Great. We're going to put Elwes in charge of your team, so you'll answer to him." I glanced across the camp at Elwes who was by that time very nearly dead, missing half an arm, and impaled very badly—or very badly impaled, whichever is correct. I nodded.

"Couldn't it be Tony Martin in charge of my project? You know Tony and I work well together."

"Martin is on Rescue Team. No, we need you here, Neal. And Kent will help you out if you have any questions." I looked

9

again at Kent; his eyes were closed and his mouth was hanging open and I was not certain that he was still alive.

That sonofabitch Randall walked off and those law students looked at me like I was a leper. Then one of them—I never caught their names—said, "This situation is messed up, Dude. Let's hike out of here and find help."

I always carry a couple of pocket-sized notebooks to keep track of things, to write little notes to myself, or to take notes on meetings I'm in. It's usually good to do that when you're an attorney, but sometimes you look back on your notes and think, "Wow, I should *not* have written that down!" Sometimes you write down extraneous things and sometimes incriminating things. I guess I was a pretty good choice to do the *Catalog of the Dead*, as much as I hate to admit it, because I'm not sure anyone else had any notebooks with them. If anyone ever read what I wrote, though, they would think that we were all monsters, probably.

None of the attorneys except for me would go back into the plane because it was so gruesome in there, so that meant I had to move all the dead bodies around by myself and reach into their pockets for their wallets and find their IDs; I got very bloody in the process and by the end of the day all my clothes stunk like blood and feces.

Yeah, feces.

The smell was bad. Pretty much everyone had lost control of their bowels when they died. It was nasty in there. But Randall, that sonofabitch, he says: "Neal, can you do this for me? I don't think anyone else can." So of course I had to. He was right, no one else would have. But it's not like it even needed to be done. I tried to explain that to him after I'd spent about an hour with the corpses, but I think he'd lost a lot of blood, or else he just wouldn't listen to me. I said: "But if they have their IDs on them, then when someone finds us they can just look at the IDs." But Randall couldn't hear me; I think he was shaken up by the crash, too, although he didn't act like it. He said that the list needed to be done and that it would just be best practices to keep track of the dead. "I get what you're saying!" I said. "But they're already kept track of! If they've got IDs on them..."

"Neal," he said. "Neal, Neal, Neal, Neal." He had his chubby little finger up in the air; he always interrupted me when I tried to speak.

"Can you please give me some help, then? Can we have Justine help me? I like working with Justine."

"Oh, I have faith you can handle this on your own. It's best practice. It needs to be done and I don't think anyone else has the stomach to do it, so we're really counting on you for this."

So, yeah, I have apparently got the strongest stomach of any attorney in the world or something. I don't like digging around dead bodies. I don't like getting blood all over me—blood that might be infected with who knows what! What offended me, though—what really offended me—wasn't that he wanted me to sift through the dead, it was that it didn't need to be done in the first place. It was a total waste of time to catalog all the dead when I should have been thinking about my own survival. There were real things that needed to be done—we needed to find a clearing in the trees, or to try to clear a spot above us; we needed to light a fire somehow that would smoke so we could be seen; we needed to clear a place on the canyon floor to sleep; we needed to find firewood; we needed to do a great many things...but one thing that absolutely did not need to be done was to write down the names of a bunch of dead people. Well, I figured, everyone else was doing the important stuff, so I'll just do this stupid catalog to get Randall off my back. It's likely that he asked me to do it to get me away from everyone else; I always got the crap work that no one else would do. Just like how I got stuck working with Will Pearson, who was about the worst partner in the entire history of things in the world. I had booked myself on this particular flight home with this crew of attorneys because Pearson was on a different flight. The firm gave life insurance policies to each of the partners, and the policies set limits on how many partners could be on a single flight, so Pearson ended up on a different flight. That's how karma gets you, though, I guess—I got stuck in this situation, even though I'm a decent sort, and Pearson, who is awful, took a nice flight home, had a nightcap, and then went to bed, or whatever it was that he did at night. That sonofabitch Randall hated me, that's why he put me in that plane to write the *Catalog of the Dead.*

It was a bleak scene inside the plane and no one in his right mind would have the stomach to go back into that plane, to work in that plane.... Hell! To live in it! Adam Billings vomited three times that I saw, just because he couldn't stand the sight of blood or something, and he wasn't even working *in* the plane. No surprise there; he had always struck me as the type that would vomit all over himself rather than go digging through the pockets of a dead body. And Jeffrey, God bless him, he started crying, and I mean full-on weeping. His body convulsed because he was crying so hard. He had a wife and new son at home and his wife was a really sweet and wonderful person, so I guess it made sense that he'd fall apart like that, knowing that he might never be able to be home with his family again. Adam and Jeffrey were young guys, like me. I think Adam was a fifth year associate. And Jeffrey and I were in our fourth years. Amy and Carla from my group were on the flight, too. Carla was just about as senior in the group as that sonofabitch Randall and she was no one to mess with, and Amy was an associate but was in her seventh or eighth year and practically a partner; she probably had already talked about partnership with the firm, so the crash was really putting an obstacle in her career development path. Carla hardly batted an eyelash after the crash; she was a tough person, the kind of person who my mother would have called a "hard woman". Amy was a little teary eyed, but that's to be expected, I guess, if you care at all about your life. And she was married, too, so her husband was out there somewhere wondering where she could be. Carla and I were about the only ones who didn't break down in some way or another directly after the crash. Maybe Carla didn't have anyone to go home to? I don't know. Everyone else was crying, to tell you the truth, even the manly men like Adam and George Barnes. I think that sonofabitch Randall might have cried, too, because he ran off to "do reconnaissance" after the crash, but I bet he used that as an excuse to go somewhere and cry because he was scared. Or maybe not, because who knows what kind of emotions a guy like that has? But even Carla would break down eventually if she stayed out there long enough. Anyone would. Don't think you wouldn't.

I set about cataloging the dead and Randall, that sonofabitch, he was rousing up team spirit outside. Some of us were injured pretty badly, like Kent Elwes—he was a good guy at work, I liked to work for him, although I'd always heard that he sexually harassed female attorneys and that's why there were so few women in our group. Eh, he seemed a good sort to me. But he was missing his arm just above the elbow and was bleeding pretty badly, and he was impaled on a rod or a shard of metal from a seat frame, so I bet that he would be the first to go if we didn't get rescued. He was pale. I'm pretty sure the crash impaled him and that he wasn't like that before.

I should get the catalog business out of the way, just for the record. I remember all the numbers even without looking at the *Catalog of the Dead*, but I don't remember all the names. Even if I did remember the names, I wouldn't write them down here because those unlucky dead folks have families out there, people who care about their memory. They wouldn't want me writing about it. Here they are, without names:

THE DEAD:
- 3 flight attendants
- 2 pilots
- 7 members of a professional soccer team
- 3 families of 4 people, 2 parents and 2 children each
- 3 families of 3, 2 parents and a child each
- 12 couples (or pairs who I thought were couples)

- 24 females flying alone, various ages
- 51 males flying alone, various ages
- 1 unidentified child, gender impossible to determine
- 2 unidentified adults, gender impossible to determine

Earlier I mentioned those three healthy young law students who made it through the crash but who weren't attorneys with our group. They chucked it after the crash and headed off down the mountain within the hour. We never heard from them again and I'm guessing they died somewhere on the mountain. Maybe—just maybe—they stopped somewhere by that clear running brook and founded an artists' colony or something. We always have to keep hope alive.

No, I'm joking. They're dead.

∞ ∞ ∞ ∞ ∞ ∞ ∞ ∞ ∞ ∞ ∞ ∞ ∞ ∞ ∞

"Neal!"

It was Amy calling to me. She was still crying lightly, so faintly that I could hear it only because the wrecked fuselage acted like an echo chamber. The fact that she was crying, but crying so lightly, made her appear stronger, like she was doing well...*all things considered.* I was in the front end of the wrecked plane extricating the dead from the accordion seating and cataloging their names for Randall, that sonofabitch. A lot of the bodies weren't in very good shape. Mostly I had to move the torsos, leave the legs behind, then clear out the seats and bags and all that from a couple rows' worth of seating just to get to the next layer of corpses. Later I tried to match up the legs with the torsos. "NEAL!"

"What?" I yelled back at her. Amy was damn close to making partner, so I had to be accommodating with her. "Something I can help you with?"

"I'm cold," she said. "It's so cold out here."

"You better not come in here," I said. "It's pretty bleak."

"What?"

"Bleak," I said. "It's bleak in here. Stay out there."

"It's cold out here. Are there any blankets?"

"Yes," I said. "I'll get you some blankets. You should start a fire."

She mumbled something that I could not hear. She didn't know how to start a fire, I'd imagine, because nobody knows how to do that anymore, and the Fire Team had totally failed so far. No one had a cigarette lighter—not because attorneys don't smoke, but because they were all afraid to try to carry a lighter through the TSA stop. I'm no dummy, though, so I looked through the corpses until I found someone who I thought looked like a smoker and then I checked her pockets. Nothing. So while I was looking for blankets for Amy, I pulled some bags out from the overhead bin that I thought must have been the bin around the same place in the plane that the smoker lady would have been sitting. It was tough to guess where that would have been, though, because the plane was pretty jacked up and some of the overhead bins had fallen down. There were three lighters in the first bag I checked. So I pocketed them.

"Here you go," I said. I handed blue blanket after blue blanket out through the gash of the plane. Amy took them one by one and put them in a pile because she was going to distribute them. Then that sonofabitch Randall walked over.

He was a fat tumor of a man, as malignant as he was paunchy. He was limping because his leg got messed up in the crash and his funny limp made the big gobbler of fat under his chin sway back and forth as he walked.

"Got phone reception, Neal?" he asked me.

"I haven't checked," I said.

"You haven't checked? You haven't CHECKED?"

"Been cataloging the dead for you," I said. "There are a lot of dead. Anyway, my phone's AT&T, so...."

"We're hidden here, Neal," he said. He waved his hands around at the sky, or at what blocked us from the sky. "We can't see the sky—no one can see us. Do you understand that? I sometimes wonder if you understand the gravity and severity of this situation. Do you?"

"Yes," I said. And I did! Perhaps I understood the gravity and severity of the situation more than my colleagues.

"A cell phone might be our only link to the outside world. Do you get it? Am I being clear enough on that point for you to understand?"

"I understand that," I answered, and spoke slowly. I always found that you had to speak slowly with attorneys because they are always certain that you're confused and they aren't; often it's the other way around.

"Well then don't you think you should have checked your phone reception, Neal?"

"I don't think you understand *me*," I said, still speaking slowly so that he could follow along. "I mean, I understand that it would be beneficial for people in a situation like ours to have a strong connection to the outside world. In fact, I'd bet that every single person *here* understands that almost on an instinctual level. Indeed, the idea crossed my mind almost as soon as we crashed that, "you know what: It might be good to be able to call for help!" Because I'm not a fucking idiot...."

"Do you think you might be able to check your cell phone reception for all of us?" he asked me. Oh, but he was condescending. He was a Napoleonic little twerp of a fat man. Randall never had liked me, not one bit. It's a mystery why he'd hired me in the first place, because he disliked me so much. I'd been working with him personally (and Pearson, remember?) for the past several months on a bear of a project—stupidest project ever, but that's neither here nor there. Nothing I ever did at work was right, nothing was ever good enough or complete enough or concise enough for him. The thought crossed my mind that he'd maybe hired me on a lark because he liked having people around to fire if the time came and he had a bad day or if something awful happened and they needed to fire *someone*. That happens all the time at big law firms, and I bet it happens at just about every big business, because it happens in life all the time: People who aren't to blame take the blame.

"Has everyone else checked their phone reception?" I asked.

"Yes," he answered. Amy picked up the blankets and walked away.

"And is everyone here on fly-by-night independent cell providers, or are they perhaps on AT&T?"

"I don't know, Neal," he answered.

"I'd bet you that someone here has AT&T and has checked their phone for service. And the firm's BlackBerries are on AT&T, I know for a fact. And, to be clear, *my service is also AT&T*. So it seems likely that someone has already turned on their phone to check for nearby cell towers. It follows, then, that it would probably be a waste of time and a waste of my battery for me to check mine. But if you think that it's more important for me to check my phone—even though I know that it will not have any service—than to work on the *Catalog of the Dead* for you...."

"If you have time, could you? If you have time. Just let me know, let's say, before the end of today? Does that work for you?" he asked me.

"Sure. I'll let you know."

∞ ∞ ∞ ∞ ∞ ∞ ∞ ∞ ∞ ∞ ∞ ∞ ∞ ∞ ∞

Moving dead bodies around is a difficult job of work and I got tired. I went to the gash in the back of the plane when I started getting tired that day—you know, for some air—and I must have fallen asleep while I sat in the eye-shaped opening. Everyone else must have fallen asleep, too. We were all tired. The crash was tiring business, just like all stressful things. When I finally woke up I thought it was the next day, or maybe even two days later. It was light outside. Almost everyone was asleep on the cold ground in a dog pile of attorneys. Jeffrey wasn't sleeping, though, and I could hear him still bawling. Man, he broke down on impact. It would have been best for all of us if we got rescued that day, but it looked like it was really important for Jeffrey. He just couldn't handle it. I didn't know if he would be able to go on living if we didn't get rescued that day. It looked like he might actually die of a broken heart or whatever the medical term for what he was going through.

His crying got worse that day, too, because we heard search planes all day long. The search planes were small, not like the big 737 that nearly killed us, and we could hear their tiny engines whining high above us. Sometimes they zoomed over quite near where we were and all of us would yell and yell to try to get their attention and we'd run down to the stream and yell and yell, but no one could hear us or see us because of the trees and because we'd wedged so tightly into such a slim canyon. Hearing those search planes destroyed Jeffrey because he just kept getting his hopes up that he'd be back with his wife and kids but then losing faith again when the planes circled over us and flew back out of earshot. Planes have those black boxes in them, you know the ones that send out rescue signals? Ours didn't work. Only time in history that the black box has failed, so I hear. Big lawsuit about that now.

I gave that sonofabitch Randall one of the cigarette lighters I'd found, but I guess he couldn't get a fire going. Maybe the wood was too moist. But he was furious with his Fire Team, so he told them all to find other tasks and he put Jeffrey in charge of gathering wood for a rescue fire and for a fire to keep them all warm at night, just in case they ever got a fire started. Jeffrey was still bawling constantly, but Randall thought that he'd do better if he kept busy. The nights were going to be cold and black.

I got word later that day that Denny Simons was dead. His death surprised us all because he looked as healthy as can be—I thought he'd come through the crash without any injuries like Justine and I had, but then he just died without warning. There must have been internal injuries. He was a good guy. Just one year ahead of me in the firm. Simons was a superstar attorney; he had two partners who adored him and so he billed about 3200 hours the year before he died, and those are solid hours for a fifth year associate. He was a great guy, too, and we had a lot in common. He was a gear-head, like I was when I was younger, and we used to talk about cars; he had a 1976 Cosworth Vega that he'd restored and I was jealous of that. We'd had a lot of drinks together in the airport right before the crash and he was telling me how excited he was that he was starting to get some time to spend with his wife and their daughter. He planned to do two more years, really push it for big bonuses, and then he was going to leave because his wife was going to Le Cordon Bleu and he had an MBA so they were going to open up a bistro somewhere. I thought that was a silly dream, but it wasn't my dream, so who am I to judge? Most of us had dreams or fantasies about what we would do once we got out of the firm and I bet we would all be embarrassed to have the world know our little dreams or to see them splashed up on a screen. I shouldn't share that kind of stuff, that kind of really personal, dreamy stuff about these folks. I'll try not to. But know that we all had our dreams. I had my dreams, too.

No one acted scared that day when Denny died, but I think we all were scared—if Denny could go like that even though he looked so healthy, then maybe any of us could. I imagine that we each worried that day that we might have internal injuries; I know I worried. It was a scary day.

"Neal!"

This was Carla yelling at me. She was a nice lady, but I would rather it had been Amy or even Jeffrey because Carla was harsh and intimidating. I was really pulling for Jeffrey, but he was broken down, so I guess Carla was looking for someone else to help her with things that needed done.

"Yes?"

"Can you come down here?"

"Sure," I said.

I climbed out of the plane. It was nice to be out because the bodies were starting to stink by that time. (The stink would get a lot worse.) I'd decided to break out each of the plane's windows that I could because of the smell and because there would be methane and noxious gasses to worry about as the dead started to decompose. The broken windows helped a little with the stink, but it was still dank and awful in there. It was nice to be outside. Amy had been right about the temperature: it was cold outside the plane. I wondered how they'd all made it through the night. They must have all snuggled up close together under the blankets. Cuddling isn't natural for attorneys, so I bet they all hated that.

"Did you add Denny's name to the list?" she asked me. Now, don't think she was coarse like this because of the crash. She was like that all the time. She never had started conversations with things like "How the hell are you?" or "Good weekend?" She always got right to business.

"No," I said.

"You should," Carla said.

"Why? I mean, we know who he is."

"The list should contain all of the dead, don't you think?"

"I'm not entirely sure of that," I answered. "I already mentioned to Randall that I'm not a hundred per cent sure that we need to even bother with this list. And, anyway, it's Randall's list."

"Randall!" she called. Fat tumor Randall waddled over. He did a great job of hiding his injuries, but he was really not doing well and I saw that one of his legs was maybe even broken. That's why he limped so funny and his gobbler flopped. "Randall, Neal thinks we shouldn't add Denny's name to the list."

"Of course we should," Randall said. "The list should be complete. It should be concise, and it should be accurate, but most of all it should be complete. And concise. We need to keep track of everyone."

"Denny's got ID on him," I said. "And we all know him. We know and can verify that body right over there for the authorities...that it belongs to Denny. So if we make it out...."

"WE WILL MAKE IT OUT," Randall said. He smacked his fist against the fuselage of the plane four times, one for each word in "Will. Make. It. Out."

"Well when we do make it out, we can tell people that Denny's body is right over there. *If* none of us make it...."

23

"Neal," he scolded me.

"Look, Man, we have to consider the possibility that none of us make it, we have to consider that. We have to consider the possibility that no *one will save us.* We might have to consider the possibility that we might have to save ourselves."

"No," he said. "We will make it out of this. There's the National Forest Service. Coast Guard. The military, the police. There's no way the federal government would give up and leave us out here. And, even if they did, there are search and rescue units in the private sector. One of these search groups will find us. The other is not an option. It's just not a realistic option, Neal, that the world would leave us out here to die!" Then he smiled really broadly like everything was absolutely fine.

"Well," I said. "In some alternate universe with much stricter mortality laws, then when people finally find this plane, there will be ID on Denny's body."

"What is the difference between Denny and the others?" he asked me. "Is Denny somehow better or worse than the others? Does he not deserve to be on the list because he's one of us? Or maybe he's too good for the list because he's one of us? Is there some reason why he shouldn't be included on the list?"

"Yes!" I said. "Because the list itself is a waste of time!"

"But think of the time you're wasting arguing with me about this, Neal? It's a big waste of time to argue with me. And it doesn't show the kind of team spirit or *espirit d'corps* that we need in this firm."

"This isn't the office, Randall. We're in a different reality right now."

"Just add him to the list, Neal. I know it's a hassle, but I really appreciate it. By the way, did you ever check the reception on your phone?"

"No," I said. "I didn't."

"But you told me you were going to check your phone?"

"No. I *said the words* that I was going to check my phone, but clearly by the inflection in my voice I was telling you that I was *not* going to check my reception."

"Can you check it now? I mean, you have time now, right? Do you have something else to do?"

"Look!" I said. I yanked the phone out of my pocket and turned it on. It was going to be a very dramatic moment! But it wasn't because we had to wait like two minutes for the damn phone to boot up. I had over 80% of battery left on my phone.

"Huh!" I said. "I had thought there might be service on my phone and *only* on my phone. But it looks like there isn't and that the laws of physics have held constant with regard to my unique cell phone."

"Well, best keep checking every hour or so," Randall said. "Keep me updated."

I added Denny to the *Catalog of the Dead.*

∞ ∞ ∞ ∞ ∞ ∞ ∞ ∞ ∞ ∞ ∞ ∞ ∞

Kent died in the night from his injuries. It was no surprise. His death *was* shocking for everyone out there, though, even if it came as no surprise. No one could handle it. It hit people hard that time not because Kent was especially well loved, or liked even, but that he was the second one of us to die. Simons, then

Kent. That's two people, Man. Two real live human people and like 7% or 8% of our entire practice group. Just dead. So I could hear the living ones bawling outside the plane as I was finishing up my work for the day. One of the women, I think it was Justine, was crying and Jeffrey was wailing. "Oh, no, no," he wailed, "God, no!" and "WHY? WHY? GOD WHY!?"

It was a night of lamentations. It's not likely that any of us had ever even seen a dead body before, except at a funeral, and here were two of our own as dead as posts to add to the 120 or so that I'd already added to the *Catalog of the Dead*. Kent's face was pale and his mouth was open. Just ghastly. The sobbing and the crying were awful and that sonofabitch Randall wasn't saying or doing anything about it. Randall just sat over there by the woods in his little spot where he could watch everyone and he pretended to be deep in thought. Who knows what that tumor of a man was thinking about, his thick fat hands pressed together and propping up his gobbler. All the howling and crying got to me, Man. Two deaths I can handle, but all the bawling! These people were practically ululating by this time—I just didn't want to listen to it anymore. They were obviously in great emotional pain and were unable to do anything about it. So I climbed out of the plane, picked up Kent's body and carried it off into the woods back behind Randall. Then I went back for Denny's body and carried it away into the woods. I lay the bodies side-by-side and covered them up with leaves and bark and debris off the forest floor. I found as many big stones as I could, too, and stacked those on top of and around their graves. It wasn't much of a burial, but it was something.

Everyone, even the lowest of the low—I mean the lowest, like killers and rapists and corrupt politicians—even they should get a decent burial. Life is hard, Man. And funerals aren't even for the dead, anyway; a funeral is for the living. I wished I could have done more for Kent and Denny, but it was all I could do. And it stopped all my colleagues from bawling for a while. Once the bodies were out of sight, I guess, their deaths were out of mind. And with death out of mind, maybe it gave my colleagues some hope of their own.

I added Kent to the *Catalog of the Dead.*

∞ ∞ ∞ ∞ ∞ ∞ ∞ ∞ ∞ ∞ ∞ ∞

I spent most of my time in the plane with all the dead passengers. After I pulled all the bodies out from the tangle of seating, I stacked the busted seats and seat frames on one side of the plane near the gash in the back and then I tried to organize the bodies (or what used to be bodies) on the other side of the plane, right up near the cockpit door. I thought it would be nice to keep the bodies all together, I guess, and I like order. I like it when things are put in their places at the end of the day. I kept myself pretty busy cleaning up the mess in there and cataloging the dead, so I was in the plane most of the days and then it became easier and more comfortable for me to just sleep in there, too, right by the gash where fresh air came in. I crawled out to go to the bathroom, of course. And a couple of times a day I would crawl out to check on everyone, but they mostly wouldn't talk with me. At first it was because they were disgusted with me—I know that now, that they were disgusted with me because of the time I spent in the plane with the corpses. That was beneath them. None of them would even dream of going back into that plane unless some necessity forced them to, like to eat or something, and even then some of them might not have had the stomach for it. It's not that I'm strong or a Superman, it's just that we all have different weaknesses, that's all that is. They weren't talking to me, but they weren't talking much at all by the end of the week, not even to each other. Justine would still talk to me, but that goes without saying. Justine and I were pretty tight. The truth is that I had a crush on Justine for a long time. I had never told her about it, though, because you don't say that kind of stuff to your co-workers. Plus, she was married. And I was engaged. So it's just best to not say that kind of thing in the workplace.

Just about every time I came out to walk around and get some fresh air, Randall or Carla would pull me aside and ask for something else from inside the plane. They wanted blankets, then they wanted pillows, and then they wanted to know about the radio. As the days went by, I could tell how the group's collective state of mind was by the things they asked me to find on the plane—on good days, they asked me to check it again for food, and on the bad days they asked me to check it for parachutes, collapsible bicycles, really crazy stuff that I guess they thought would aid in their rescue. They asked for skis once. Like planes have an extra set of skis on them? I imagined my colleagues out there making fantastic escape plans—first we ski down the canyon until we find a cliff and then we fashion a parachute or a winged flying suit from tarpaulin from the plane and then we leap from the cliff and land safely near a military installation. There was always something they needed and I was the only one who would go into the plane, so they needed me.

The business of extricating and cataloging the dead took quite a bit of my time at first. There were like a hundred bodies in that plane, all mangled and tangled and stuck in between seats. I rooted through all the passengers' bags for valuables. There were a lot of electronics that were all useless to me. But I found a pretty sweet knife hidden in the bag of an outdoorsy looking fellow with a beard who had been cut up pretty badly in the crash; he also had a copy of a book called *The Treasure of the Sierra Madre*, by B. Traven, so I had something to read. I love that book now, but maybe that's just because I discovered it after the crash and it kept me company. The best thing I found was a big bag of raisins that I kept and had a couple of raisins as a treat every now and again, but later I gave the bag of raisins to Justine. I kept all the valuables in the cockpit for safekeeping, because I didn't trust my colleagues. So, because all the corpses were down there, I had to move them out of the way every time I had to get in the cockpit. It was the only way I could be sure to keep the lawyers away from the valuable stuff I stored in there.

Tough job. Really hard work, Man.

I could hear them outside when they talked, but as the days went by they talked less and less. When they talked, it was usually about the strategy to get saved—whether to hike out or wait.

"We *have* to leave, Randall, or send some of us *away*," Carla said. She was the only person there who could stand up to Randall.

"We can't," he said. "If we wait, someone will come to find us. And when we get rescued, what would it look like if we'd sent some of us out of here? We have to consider the reputational risk."

"But we'll run out," she said. "We'll run out of food and water and fire...."

"Fire Team is carrying *its* weight," Randall said. He was getting angry. "We'll be OK if we just wait this out. We can't leave, Carla, because we don't know where we are. Look at this forest! Look at it!"

He didn't talk like that with associates. With us, he was more condescending, but with partners he was almost confrontational.

"Randy," she said. "This is...we're in a bad situation."

"I think Randall is right," Amy offered. "Who knows how far the forest goes on? Who knows if we could even *find* our way out? And if we were to send someone out, who would we send? How would we choose who to send? And what might happen to them out there?"

Sometimes they argued about the stream nearby, about whether the water was clean or safe to drink, even though it was the only water they had access to for drinking water, so they had no choice about what to drink or whether to drink from the stream. Sometimes they argued about how to start a fire even though they had a cigarette lighter. They practically all had heart attacks and sang choruses when Jeffrey finally got a fire started. Jeffrey pulled himself together, you know, and really came into his own out there after his initial little break with reality.

When I got tired of moving dead bodies or doing pointless searching in the plane for this-or-that thing Carla or Randall wanted, I'd lay down by the gash in the plane so that my head could hang out of the plane and I could smell fresh air. Justine used to come and sit by the plane and talk to me. Back at the office, it was usually the other way around—I'd stop by her office and we'd talk.

Justine Moore was the prettiest thing out there for several miles around, I think. She was a great person. She had a good heart, was a good person. We liked to laugh together. Back at the firm, I'd usually get stuck in her office for an hour or more laughing and joking about how sad and pathetic our lives were. And it was the same out there. Justine and I laughed about how badly we smelled and how tired and hungry we were, about how we hadn't slept well. We laughed about all sorts of stuff. Funny stuff happened out there after the crash. You don't think you'd laugh, but you learn to find humor in things, and the more desperate the situation then the more you can find humor in darkness. Mostly we laughed at how that sonofabitch Randall argued about everything and bossed everyone around and at how no one could start a fire. Oh, Billings! My God, did we laugh at Billings.

Adam Billings spent three or four days trying to build a snare to catch wild game and that was a laugh riot. Billings was an asshole; just a horrible guy. His head was huge—I mean physically he had a large head—and he was pretty good looking, so he looked like some WASPy movie star. He laughed too loud and drank too much, too.

Ok, so, yes, I was in love with Justine Moore. You fall in love with people in situations like that. I'd had a crush on her before the crash, but it was just an innocent thing. But I fell in love with her out there.

"Look at Billings," she'd say to me. We'd look over and see Billings fiddling with bits of string or sticks. "I bet this is the one. This is the snare. He'll get a squirrel with that."

"Are you sure? He might get a rabbit."

"Or a bobcat?"

"He might snare an antelope," I'd say.

"He's such a provider!" she'd coo.

We'd watch him over there with his brow furrowed in thought; he'd hold up a rock in one hand and a couple of sticks in the other, as if by staring at them hard enough he could will them into the shape of a snare or a deadfall trap. It was like a sitcom for Justine and me. Stupid Billings would work on the deadfall trap and someone, usually Kwame or Givens, would come over and plop down next to him.

"Whatcha makin'?"

"A deadfall trap," Billings would say. "I saw Bear Grylls do this."

"Oh!"

About that time the rock would fall and crush his thumb and Billings would curse and bounce around and blow on his thumb as if that would make it feel better. Then an announcer would say "Thaaaat's Billings!" and the theme song would come on and the crowd would laugh.

Doesn't seem funny now. Not even to me.

But that's funny stuff when you're in a desperate situation.

And it's sexy when someone smiles. That's the sexiest to me, when someone is happy in a desperate situation. And it's not like either of us were happy while we were stranded, but it's sexy when someone can keep themselves grounded in bad situations and can still smile. And "happy" isn't the right word—it's not about happiness or unhappiness, really, it's just desperation. Justine and I were both so desperate that "desperation" was the only emotion we had time for. Were we unhappy? Eh, the question doesn't make sense. We were just desperate. And I dig strength in desperate times. It's probably not healthy—I have always had weird fascination for strength in desperate times. Like when I was a kid and my grandpa told stories about the Great Depression, I always wondered how I would do in the same circumstances. I always wondered what it would feel like to be tested. So, yeah, I fell in love with her. Maybe she fell in love with me, too. But she was married and we were all going to die, anyway, so it was never meant to be.

∞ ∞ ∞ ∞ ∞ ∞ ∞ ∞ ∞ ∞ ∞ ∞ ∞

ACT II: THE LAWYERS

By the 9th or 10th day I started to think of the other attorneys as "The People Outside the Plane". I even lumped Justine into that category in my mind, even though I was in love with her. I hardly ever left the plane anymore except to go to the bathroom and maybe once a day to walk a bit in the open air. I fashioned a little heat stove in the plane near the rear bathrooms and made a chimney out of thick cloth that I built to run out of one of the windows. I couldn't have a very big fire in there because the cloth chimney would have caught fire, but I was able to keep warm with very little fuel. There were plastic bottles of various sizes on the plane, too, so I passed some of them out to the People Outside the Plane and kept a few for myself and stored water in them.

It was about the 10th or 11th day when the People Outside the Plane started to get hungry. Like really hungry. Randall or Carla sent Jeffrey over to me to ask to search the plane for food about a thousand times.

"Hey, Buddy," he'd say, then lean against the plane. "You got a few minutes?"

"Maybe," I said. I'd lean out of the plane to talk with him and sometimes even step out for some air. It was still safe at that time.

"Randall has a research project and I'm swamped on Fire Team. Think you could look through the plane for food?"

"I'm busy on the *Catalog of the Dead*," I said. "Randall put me on the *Catalog* project right after we crashed. So, you know, my days are pretty full right now. You can come on the plane and look, if you'd like?"

He wouldn't. No one else would go onto that plane because of the bodies and the stink.

Each time Jeffrey came to the plane, I offered to help him onto the plane to look, but he would never come on. After a few attempts, I guess they figured that Jeffrey wasn't the right person to talk with me, so they sent Amy over. Again, I said that I was awfully busy on the *Catalog* project, but that she could come onto the plane and look if she wanted to. She wouldn't. Then Carla came to the plane, and I knew things were getting serious because Carla was a big-time partner, second in command to Randall, really. I offered to help Carla onto the plane, too, but she wouldn't come up there.

Eventually, even Randall himself came to me for gruesome assistance as time was running out for the People Outside the Plane.

"Can you search the plane for food?" Randall asked.

"I could search the plane again," I said.

"But you already have searched the plane?"

"Yes," I said.

"But can you search it again? For *food?*" And he emphasized the word "food". Randall did not blink and did not break his malignant stare; I was standing inside the plane, right at the gash, and I could turn and look back into the darkness of the plane, but I could also see out over the campsite where the People Outside the Plane were living and sleeping. I do not know why, even now, but I knew that Randall could not bring himself to come into the plane and that I was safe in there. I think it was for fear that he'd lose prestige among the other attorneys. He said it again.

"Neal, search the plane and bring us *food.*"

I knew what he was asking me to do. He was asking for the bodies. They weren't interested in actually searching the plane for food by that time—they were after the bodies, and they were only using the phrase *"search the plane for food"* so that they wouldn't have to face their own grim reality.

"No," I said.

"Neal, I'm not going to ask you again. You do this for me and I'll remember it. But if you don't...."

"No," I said. "I'm not going to do that. And I'm not going to let you do that, either."

Looking back, that was the end of my working relationship with Randall and with the firm. You can't say *no* like that.

He swallowed hard and I could see the muscles of his jaw clench and release. His jaw muscles were large and well developed beneath the soft layers of his fat face. He was getting weak by that time and he leaned against the plane to stay standing; he didn't let on, but Randall wasn't feeling well at all because he hadn't eaten. The People Outside the Plane were restless, weak, and hungry. I decided then that I would not, under any circumstances, let them in to where all the bodies were.

I felt fine, to tell you the truth. I didn't feel hungry or thirsty or tired or anything; I'd settled into quite a nice routine inside the plane. I gave thanks every day I was managing so well because I didn't think I could ever eat a human being. I just didn't think I could do that, no matter how dire the situation. I would probably die if it came to that. But it was about to come to that—anyone could see it. And I started to worry for Muhammed and Lance Givens, because neither of them was doing very well. Denny Simons had died really quickly, so that was good for him because no one was hungry enough at the time to even think about it. Then Elwes died and his body bloated up and started rotting while the People Outside the Plane bawled and argued so I took the initiative, left the plane, and carried the corpses away from the People Outside the Plane. They probably would have argued and cried for days while the things rotted right beside them; eventually they would have broken down, though. The People Outside the Plane were becoming disgusting people. But, then again, I was living and working in a cave of corpses, so who am I to judge?

The first one would have to go of natural causes. I was certain of that. The People Outside of the Plane would never do anything rash without precedent, not even that sonofabitch Randall. So the first one would have to go natural. But after that it might not be safe to fall asleep.

∞ ∞ ∞ ∞ ∞ ∞ ∞ ∞ ∞ ∞ ∞ ∞ ∞

"Neal!" It was Carla.

"Yeah!" I said and poked my head out of the plane.

"Do you know CPR or anything? Is there another first aid kit on the plane?"

"I can look," I said.

"Look? Shouldn't you *know* by now? Isn't it your job to *know* what's on the fucking plane? What have you been doing in there?"

"Well, I'm drafting a *Catalog of the Dead*. Randall asked me to," I said. "It's taking a lot longer than I thought it would."

"How many dead are there on the plane?"

"Lots," I said. "Quite a few. It's bleak in here."

"We need a first-aid kit. Jesus, Neal. Is there another first aid kit?"

"No."

"Are you sure?" she asked me.

"Yes, I'm positive. I've been over every inch of this plane."

"Can you look again?"

"I can look again, but there isn't another one on board. What do you need?"

"Medicine. Givens isn't doing well."

"I'll check passenger's bags, too," I said. That seemed to satisfy her. So I spent a few hours going back through all the passenger's bags looking for medicine. I'd been through all the bags so many times that I knew there wasn't anything useful there, but I told her that I would so I did.

I didn't find anything useful. No one carries useful medicine in carry-on bags. It didn't really matter because Givens was going to die with or without medicine. I knew that. Everyone should have known that. The kid weighed 90 pounds when we got on the plane. He was a first year associate and I didn't much care for him, anyway. He was a real cutthroat, the kind of slimy guy that would smile at you while he had his hand in your pocket. He probably would have gone on to be the managing partner eventually. And he weighed, seriously, about 140 pounds soaking wet; he was sickly thin even before the crash because all he ever did was work for that sonofabitch Randall. So he couldn't make it long without food and being all banged up from the crash.

I came back out and said, "Nope. No medicine." Then Carla left and I sat in the gash of the plane. Justine was nearby and she came over. I jumped out and we sat together, leaning our backs against the wreckage.

"I'm scared," Justine told me.

"Don't be," I said. "No need."

"No need? You don't think?"

"It's no use borrowing troubles," I said. "My mom always said that. It's no use borrowing troubles." I smiled for her and hoped that would help. I doubt it did, at least not much.

"I'm worried about Givens. And I'm really scared."

"Don't be," I said again.

"We can't go on without food, can we?" she asked. I shook my head. "And you know what they'll do. You know what they'll do when they get hungry enough."

"You won't?"

"Never."

∞ ∞ ∞ ∞ ∞ ∞ ∞ ∞ ∞ ∞ ∞ ∞

You think you know people after you've worked with them for 15 hours a day. After you've been to their houses. After you'd seen them at their worst at midnight, having worked two days straight. But George Barnes surprised me. Now, I liked George Barnes. He and I got along really well, even though he was a real manly-man, hunter and golfer and scotch drinker, and I normally don't pal around with those types on account of my not being interested in that kind of thing. Barnes had some faults, but we all do. He wasn't much to talk to, that's true, but he was a hell of a good attorney. He was just one year ahead of me, so we knew each other pretty well. Or I thought we did.

"Neal, we have to talk," he said. "Can I come in there?"

"In the plane?" I asked.

"Yes."

"Well...yes, I guess. If you want to." There's not a lot of room in a situation like that to trust people. Barnes wasn't the kind of person to lie to your face, though, and I could tell that he really wanted to talk with me because something was bothering him. So I wasn't afraid of him at all in that moment.

He climbed into the plane.

"I need you to promise me something," he said.

"What's that?"

He kept turning to look out of the plane to make sure that no one could hear him talking. But no one was paying attention, because no one paid any attention to what happened inside the plane.

"I need you to promise me that you'll take care of my body if I die. Like you did the others."

His face was turning green from the stench in the plane, and we were standing right beside the gash. Hell, half of his body was in the light of the canyon, so he was hardly in the plane at all, but that goes to show how awful and thick the smell was in there.

"Carry me away. Or stick me in here with the others. But you can't let them get at my body."

"Ok," I said.

"I'm serious," he said. And he was serious. I could see it in his face that he was gravely serious. "We don't have any food, Neal."

"I know."

"And we can't go on like this," he added. "Not without any food. Not without anything to eat."

"I know that."

"If we're going to live, you know what we're going to have to do?"

"The thought crossed my mind," I said.

"That can't happen to me, Neal. Promise me that it won't? I'm sick. I'm not sick...I've just.... It's under control with medication. It's a long story."

"You don't have to tell me," I said.

"I'm not ashamed of anything," he said. "So I...."

"You don't have to tell me," I said again. "Your business is your business, Barnes. But if you want me to take care of you, in the event of, then I will."

"You're a man of your word?" he asked. I nodded. "Even in situations like this? You're still a man of your word?"

"Especially in situations like this," I said.

"You can't let anyone...you know. Because I'm sick."

"I get it."

"Promise me?"

"I promise," I said. "I promise."

∞ ∞ ∞ ∞ ∞ ∞ ∞ ∞ ∞ ∞ ∞ ∞ ∞

It was the night before Givens, I remember, and the fire had burnt down to embers, so it was late at night. All the People Outside the Plane were sleeping around the fire, or were at least pretending to be asleep.

"They're going to eat Givens," Justine said. She didn't even whisper. All the People Outside the Plane were so hungry and tired that they could hardly hear and she was so hungry and tired that she could hardly talk above a whisper anyway. "They all decided."

"Even Tony?" I asked.

"I don't know, Neal. I know Randall and Carla and Amy decided. Just as soon as Givens is dead. They talked about it like he wasn't even there. They're going to eat him."

"I won't do that," I said.

"I can't do it," she said. "I can't do it."

"I couldn't, either," I told her. "I'd die if it came to that." I had the strangest notion that I should brush her hair back with my hand, so I did, and she smiled at me. Her hair was matted with campfire smoke and dirt. We both smelled awful and I was half hanging out of a plane full of dead bodies. So it wasn't the most romantic moment.

"I'm leaving," she said. "I'm going to leave and follow the stream."

"Really? You should have gone sooner," I said. I shouldn't have lectured her like that. "You should have gone off when you were stronger, before all of this. We're all so much weaker now. If you *stay*...."

"I didn't go earlier because I thought someone would save us. I couldn't stop hoping that someone would save us. But I'm scared as hell now, Neal. I don't know how to get out of here—this forest could be as big as Connecticut for all I know. I've never even been camping. Can you believe that? I grew up in the city, Neal, and so did my husband. We're not camping people. I don't like the outdoors. But it's either go now or eat Givens," she said. "And I'm not going to eat Givens. He's got a wife at home. Look at him sleeping. He has no idea. He is an ass, but he's got a wife. He doesn't deserve to die, to be eaten, to not see it coming."

"He's a smart kid," I corrected her. "He knows it's coming. He has to know."

"That's not the point."

"I know," I said.

"Come with me?"

"I can't," I said. "I think we should stay here. We've got water here and wood for heat. We need to wait until someone finds us. If we move, they won't be able to...."

"Come with me?"

"I can't," I said again. I tried to make it sound like an apology. "I made promises out here."

"Do you think someone will come get us?"

"I don't know," I said. "I think there might be people looking for us? Anyway, I've got this *Catalog* to work on."

"Neal, think of what's going to happen here. Think of it. I can't make you come, but I think that you should come with me. Of course I'm being selfish about that, a little."

"You don't *have* to go, Justine. If you're that scared, you could stay here with me. I wouldn't let anything happen to you."

Maybe you won't believe this, but it was a tender, almost sweet moment between us. Maybe not really, but it felt like it to me. I wanted to tell her that I loved her. So I did, because that's the kind of guy that I am.

"Before you go, you should know that I'm in love with you, is the thing," I said. "It might just be our situation, though."

"Were you in love with me before the crash?"

"No," I said.

"Yeah, probably just the situation."

"Probably."

"I'm in love with you, too," she said. "Just to be clear."

"Good. That's good. Were you before the crash?"

"No," she said. "Not a bit."

"Yeah, me neither," I told her. I kind of hoped that she wasn't lying to me, but I know that she was. That's the kind of thing you lie about in situations like this. Little lies like that—just words—can mean a lot to people and don't cost you anything. So in times of crisis, I think sometimes that it's ok to lie to people about things like love and hope.

"You're a great guy. Don't get me wrong," she said.

"You, too, you're great. It's not that you aren't. It's just that before the crash, you know, I just wasn't in to you."

"I get it," she said. "I totally get that."

"When are you leaving?"

"Morning?"

"That's best practice," I said. "You can make it out of here. Send help back. Follow the water. Don't travel in the dark. And you'll have to leave before these sonsofbitches wake up. They'd never let you go."

"I know," she said. "I'm counting on you to wake me up. Neal?"

"Yes," I said.

"I need you to wake me up. If I don't make it out tomorrow morning, then I won't get out of here at all. Ever."

"I wouldn't let them get to you."

"But they will," she said. "Givens is sick, but after that.... I can't make it here. I have to go, and I need you to wake me up so that I can get out before they see me."

"I will," I said.

"Neal?"

"Yes?"

"I will probably die, won't I? I mean, most likely, I'm going to die."

"Yes," I said. "But most likely we all will. Eventually."

"I'm not going to eat Givens. Or Muhammed. And Muhammed's next after me."

"You think?"

"Yes," she said. "He's injured. No one likes him anyway."

"Yeah," I agreed. "I kind of like Muhammed. Anyway, I won't let you eat Givens."

She slumped down alongside the plane and pulled her blankets over her and I held her hand until she fell asleep. Then I climbed out of the plane and knelt beside her and I knelt there like that all night long because I knew I wouldn't fall asleep if I were kneeling. Shortly before dawn I climbed back into the plane and I found a plastic jug for her so that she could carry water on her great escape. I also gave her the bag of raisins that I'd been hoarding and eating as treats. Then I packed one of the passenger's backpacks with the bag of raisins, the plastic jug for carrying water, and a few pieces of clothing that I thought might help. I only had the one blanket for myself, but I gave her that, too, because she'd need it. I gave her one of my lighters, too, and I also gave her the sweet knife that I'd taken off of that guy. (So then I only had a little jack knife that I got off of one of the flight attendants.) I stuffed the copy of the *Treasure of the Sierra Madre* in there, too, because I thought she might like to have something to read. Or, I don't know, maybe it would be good kindling for her to start a fire. I gave her one of those flip-top pocket notebooks that I always carry, too, so she could keep a journal on

47

her way out, or whatever, and I put that in a plastic bag because it could get wet otherwise. There were several trash bags in the plane so I tossed in a few of those—she'd know to use those to keep warm and dry, I thought. There was a length of metal about 50 or 52 inches long, too, and I gave her that in the morning to use as, I don't know, a walking stick or a club or a spear. I also gave her my cell phone in the same plastic bag as the notebook—it was the only cell phone out there that might have had some battery power left because I hadn't drained it all the first day looking for a signal. It was still probably dead from having sat so long, but whatever—we were all probably dead from having sat so long. I knelt there all night long and tried not to watch her sleep like some creepy guy. I woke her before the Sun came up and I walked with her down to the stream.

"Good luck, Neal," she said.

"You'll make it," I told her. "You'll make it out of here, find a road, find a town, find a way and you'll make it. You've got to get back to your husband. You'll make it."

"I don't think I will."

"You will. Be strong."

This is the kind of stuff you say in situations like that and then spend the rest of your life regretting. Stuff like "be strong" and "you'll make it!" But, you know, it's like I said: In times of crisis, sometimes it's ok to lie to people about things like love and hope.

She leaned toward me like she was going to kiss me, but I couldn't have handled that. So I put my hands on her face and neck, softly, and kissed her on the forehead and then I pressed my cheek against her cheek. "You'll make it," I whispered. Then she whispered to me, "Come find me if you make it first." She turned and headed out along the stream. I hustled back to the plane and climbed inside. The People Outside the Plane didn't wake up for several hours because they were so exhausted from hunger.

Givens didn't wake up at all, ever again.

I added Givens to the *Catalog of the Dead.*

∞ ∞ ∞ ∞ ∞ ∞ ∞ ∞ ∞ ∞ ∞

"Neal!"

It was Jeffrey. Givens had been gone for two days and Jeffrey was doing very well. He had bounced back from whatever funk he'd been in and looked...well, he looked pretty damn strong, pretty happy, all things considered. It was intimidating, to tell you the truth.

"Yeah!?" I called back.

"Can you check for cigarettes on the plane?"

"You smoke?" I asked.

"Going to start," he said, and smiled at me through the gash in the plane. His teeth were nasty. My teeth were nasty, too, but for different reasons. "Jesus, Neal. It reeks in there."

"Yeah, I know. It's a miserable life. But someone has to catalog the dead. Takes forever to break these seats and seat frames free. It's tiring work moving these bodies. It's hot in here. It's hard, Man."

"Yes, we all appreciate what you're doing in there," he said. He was so relaxed.

"You do?"

"Yeah. Randall and Carla were talking about you last night. I don't think they'd mind that I told you."

"They were talking about *me?*" I asked. Here's why I was different than most associates: Most associates would love to hear that their managing partners were talking about them, but I didn't want to hear that at all. It bothered me to know that Randall and Carla had even mentioned my name. I'd rather they forgot about me. "Thankless job. So it's nice to be appreciated." Jeffrey and I were bonding, I guess.

"Are you feeling ok? Need something to eat?" he asked.

"No," I said. "No." I guess my tone pissed him off. I didn't try to accuse him, but it was difficult for me not to be accusatory after what they'd all done to Givens.

"You watch yourself. Watch your mouth, Man," he said. He was angry. Jeffrey had a tough time right after the crash, but then he had pulled out of it somehow. I wasn't sure how, but he was in top form. He was a beast.

"What?" I asked.

"We took just enough," he said. "Watch what you say. We only took a little and split it up between us. And it's not like we killed him."

I started to say something, but he wouldn't let me talk.

"I told you to watch your mouth," he said. He got right up close to me and put his pointer finger in my chest. But he wouldn't come on the plane. "Who the hell are you to judge, anyway, you Goddamn freak? I won't—*we* won't—listen to this kind of shit from a guy who lives in a morgue. Smell it in here! Jesus, Neal. Get some pride about yourself."

"What did you even do with him?" I asked. "There are bears and wolves and everything else out here."

"We thought of that," he said. "Randall and I carried it off."

"What?"

"We took a little and carried off the rest."

"But...that just means..."

"Means what?" he asked. Jeffrey was indignant and Jeffrey was an idiot. It meant that they'd just need to take another one if we were out there long enough. The People Outside the Plane were smart people; most lawyers are smart people. But most people are smart people, too, so that alone doesn't say much. But, as smart as they were, they didn't understand simple things sometimes. They took Givens's body away to let it rot instead of trying to save it in the cold or in the ground or to smoke it to preserve the meat. If they'd planned ahead, then I think they all could have lasted for weeks on Givens, probably long enough to be rescued. But they just threw it away like he didn't even matter, didn't even exist, wasn't even human; and that pretty much doomed us all. I think it would have gone very differently had they just been wise about the first one.

"Nothing," I said. "I'll look for smokes."

Later that day when I climbed out I took stock of the People Outside the Plane. I don't know how much of Givens they had eaten, but it clearly wasn't much. Probably just a mouthful a piece or something, that way they could rationalize it to themselves. They were still not doing well, so I was certain that they had not eaten much of Givens. Or, if they did, it had made them sick. Tony looked to be on his way out because I don't think he ate any of Givens, but there was a chance he might rally. That sonofabitch Randall looked to be pretty bad, too, because he had an infection in his fat leg and it was oozing out yellow. Kwame and Billings both were sitting with Carla, and that surprised me—Kwame had always worked with Carla, but Billings pretty much only ever worked with Kent and that sonofabitch Randall, so it was strange to see him spending time with Carla. I guessed that he was trying to get in with Carla because, with Kent Elwes dead, he wanted to have another partner to cozy up to.

"Did you find any smokes?" Jeffrey asked me. He was sitting by the fire with Amy and they were very close together. They'd been having sex. Not that second, of course, but it looked like they'd become...well...a couple, I guess is the word for it. That probably had something to do with how he'd pulled himself together. Maybe they'd have been a couple earlier if they'd had the energy, but I guess Givens spurred them on. They wouldn't have been so open about it in the office because they were both married, but out there they lorded it over us all, or at least lorded it over me. They made a point to kiss or to hug or, when they were fed, to do other stuff, directly in front of all of us—or most of us, at least in front of me and Kwame and Barnes.

"Yeah," I said. "They were in the pilot's chest pocket. There's blood on them." I tossed him the packet of cigarettes.

"This isn't blood, Dude. It's mud."

"No, it's dried blood," I said. "Believe me."

"No. It's mud. Understand?"

"Whatever, Man," I said.

I didn't sleep by the gash in the plane that night. Instead I huddled into the plane away from the gash. The stench was unbelievable but I couldn't bear to look out at the People Outside the Plane. I wasn't terribly scared, though, because I had a knife with me and I'd made another blunt spear out of part of one of the seat frames.

∞ ∞ ∞ ∞ ∞ ∞ ∞ ∞ ∞ ∞ ∞

Billings and I had never gotten along well. He was a pretty boy, and I'm a country type. There's nothing wrong with being a pretty boy, it's just grating to my nerves sometimes. I imagine that I got on his nerves, too. But Billings was a sort of pseudo-alpha male fellow; he had a lot of swagger and not much else, I don't think. That was Billings, in a nutshell. Whatever.

I didn't even recognize him when he came at me. His hair was all dirty and it was sticking up all over because of how greasy and dirty it was, and his face was covered in mud and dirt and grime, and his eyes were wide. Billings bared his teeth, too, like an animal. He'd just simply lost his mind, I thought. He came at me with a stick. It was more of a cudgel. He could have killed me with it.

I had only just stepped out of the plane for a brief moment, just for a second to get some air. And then crazy Billings set upon me. I thought, "Thaaaaat's Billings!"

He'd been waiting for me outside the plane, hunched down and waiting. He was seriously "laying in wait", or however they say it, like when an animal waits to ambush prey. I can only imagine what had been going through his head while he waited;

he was probably giving himself quite a pep talk, convincing himself that he could do what needed to be done, that he was a "stone-cold killer" or, as they say in the lawyer world, a "big swinging dick". However he did it, he'd managed to convince himself that he could kill me.

He swung once really, really hard and missed me and it threw him off balance. The force of the swing sent him careening over and off a little rise on the platform where they were all camped. I didn't push him. He landed head first on a rock. His body twitched several times after he landed on his head.

I watched his body twitch for only a second or two before I spun around to see what was happening behind me. Three of the People were standing in a semi-circle around me. Randall. Carla. Amy.

They had me surrounded.

"Oh my God!" Randall said. That sonofabitch. "What got into Billings?"

"This is difficult on all of us," Carla agreed. "Let's just all try to be calm right now for a moment. Neal, are you ok?"

"Yes," I said. "I'm fine."

I jumped down off the rise and grabbed Billings by the ankles. I pulled him back up onto the level of the camp. He'd fallen only a few feet, but he'd cracked his head pretty good and I think he might have broken his neck. Normally, I wouldn't have moved a body after a neck injury like that, but there were extenuating circumstances that day, in that three lawyers were looking at me like I was a pork tenderloin.

"Neal, on behalf of the firm, I am so sorry that happened," Randall said. He was full of shit. "Believe me, we'll make this right."

"Will you?" I asked.

"Yes," he said. "For now, maybe you should just get some rest. Take some time to rest and recuperate. We'll take care of Billings."

"Not a chance," I said.

"What do you mean?"

I'd picked up Billings's cudgel. I'm not a very strong guy, but I could pull Billings across the camp by his ankle. He didn't weigh much by then, having lost a lot of weight since the crash. I dragged his body over to the gash on the plane, but never turned my back fully to Randall, Carla, and Amy.

"I'm putting him in the plane," I said.

"You should really just rest," Amy said. "Really."

"I'm putting him in the plane," I said.

"Neal," Randall said to me. "You've got a lot on your plate already, Neal. We don't want you to spread yourself too thin. You should just leave Billings to us and I promise we'll see to it that he gets the best care we can provide."

I picked Billings up with my hands under his armpits and stuffed his body into the plane.

"He'll probably die," I said to the three of them, and I showed them the cudgel so that they knew that I meant business. They got the message. "But when that happens, it happens. And I'll add him to the *Catalog of the Dead*."

The three of them followed me to the door of the plane and called in a few times for me to bring Billings out. At first they were nice about it, but then they shouted that I was a damned freak and a terrorist. I have no idea what that meant, but they were out of their minds, so I don't hold it against them.

I put Billings near one of the windows that I'd broken open earlier. I tried to keep him as far away from all the corpses as possible for his own sake, but it was tight quarters in there. I knew he would probably die, but he deserved the best chance I could give him. So I pulled a t-shirt from someone's pack, soaked it in water, and put it to his lips. He didn't react so I left the soaked shirt in his hand just in case he woke and was thirsty. I was worried what it might look like to the authorities if they ever showed up, so I snuck out that night and grabbed the rock that he'd killed himself on and brought it into the plane. There was a chance he'd die, and I wanted to make sure to have all the evidence to show that I hadn't killed him—that it was an accident, which it was, when he tried to kill *me*. You have to watch your own back, you know? You have to cover your own ass in situations like that. The last thing I wanted was for authorities to find us out there and to get the idea that I'd killed Billings. In situations like that, people do what they have to do and you sometimes have to loosen your moral code just a smidge, but I didn't kill Billings and I didn't want anyone thinking that I did. It was just best practices to preserve the evidence even though he might have lived.

There was always hope that he'd make it.

Not really. I was pretty certain he would die.

He was dead the next time I checked on him.

I added Billings to the *Catalog of the Dead*.

∞ ∞ ∞ ∞ ∞ ∞ ∞ ∞ ∞ ∞ ∞

I stayed in the plane for two days, laying low. It would have been dangerous for me to go out of the plane right after the Billings incident. They'd sent him after me—I was sure of it. That meant that they were hungry and that I was a target. So I stayed inside the plane while they cooled off out there, and I waited. Maybe they would find something else to eat to hold them over. But it was so dank and nasty in there that I had to get out for some real fresh air after a couple of days. You can't imagine how awful it was inside that wreckage.

I took the cudgel with me and stepped down out of the plane. It was actually a pretty day, probably the prettiest day we'd had out there, and it felt like maybe some nice warm weather was not quite there but on its way.

The People Outside the Plane were all seated beside the fire, looking peaked and scribbling in the dirt with sticks. They had a nice fire, though.

Muhammed bin Muhammed was nervous and looked lonely. He was sitting with Tony, but he and Tony had never really worked together before. They didn't have much of a relationship, because Tony mostly only fed work to me at the firm—he didn't have a lot of work to give, and we had a good working relationship, so he didn't work with many others. The truth is that we all knew that Muhammed wouldn't last long—and I'm talking about before the Crash, here, back at the firm. He never fit in at the firm. I'll come back to him in a bit, though.

Amy and Jeffrey sat together very close on the same log with blankets over them and they were embracing underneath the blankets. Kwame and Carla sat together, but were not talking and they rarely looked up.

"Where's George?" I asked. A couple of them looked up, but they mostly didn't seem to hear me. I said it again, much louder, and held up the cudgel, "Where's George?"

Kwame looked at Muhammed, then looked at me, and then Muhammed shrugged. I did *not* want to leave the plane, but I'd made a promise, so I went into the woods. I found them pretty quickly.

They were circling a very large tree.

That sonofabitch Randall had a knife out—I hadn't even known he had a knife until then because that sonofabitch had kept it hidden. And he was chasing Barnes around the tree, trying to get at him. He'd taken Barnes away from the others so that they wouldn't know. Randall wanted all of Barnes for himself, I think. Barnes was crying and trying to explain to him that he couldn't do it, he shouldn't do it, that it wasn't safe for him.

"Goddamnit Randy! Would you listen! I have HIV!"

Randall wasn't very quick, but he was determined. I couldn't be certain whether he wasn't listening to George or whether he just didn't give a damn. He was bound and determined to kill him. I shouted:

"Randall! Leave him alone."

They both perked up because I'd surprised them.

"Leave him alone," I said.

"Neal, get back to your...."

"Leave him alone," I said again, and I held up the cudgel so he knew I meant business. He was outnumbered and he was awfully weak because he hadn't eaten much in a long time and he was a man who needed to eat. He exhaled deeply and stood straight up, let his hands fall to his sides. Barnes started to walk toward me, and just as he did, that sonofabitch Randall took a couple of quick steps forward and stuck Barnes in the gut with his knife. I raced at them and swung my cudgel. I landed a couple of good smacks against Randall's shoulders and back, but then he caught the cudgel and pulled it out of my hands. Barnes and I went running back toward the plane and that fat bastard Randall had no chance of catching us. He was strong, and he was quick as hell over the first few steps, but he was not fast.

We got to the gash into the plane and I climbed in quickly. I turned and held out my hand to Barnes, but he didn't take it. He was bleeding badly and his hands were covered in blood from trying to cover the wound. But he just looked at me.

"Nah," he said. He shook his head. "I gotta get away from the stream; away from the plane. Don't let them follow me?"

"George! Get on the plane!" I shouted. It was no use. He'd made up his mind to do the right thing, or the next best thing, or whatever it was that he called it.

He smiled and took off running. Barnes used whatever few calories he'd gotten from Givens to run away, to take himself out of the equation so that he would not, even by accident or through no fault of his own, injure someone. That's a hero in my book.

I didn't have any idea how I would keep them all from following him, but I didn't have to. They were all too tired to run and the fat man wasn't fast enough to catch him. Randall plopped back down on his throne over there and watched us all.

He would die out there from his injuries. I was positive of that. Randall had killed him.

I added Barnes to the *Catalog of the Dead*.

The bastard had my cudgel.

∞ ∞ ∞ ∞ ∞ ∞ ∞ ∞ ∞

Muhammed bin Muhammed was next to go. He hadn't eaten a bit of Givens and was weak as hell. But he damn sure wasn't going to be eaten. And because I'd made myself safe in the plane, they would have gone after him next. Tony was no friend to Muhammed. Don't get me wrong, I *liked* Tony. Tony was my favorite partner to work for. By the time we got on that damned plane after the group retreat he was about the only partner in the group who I would even work with. But despite all of Muhammed's efforts, he could never really get close to Tony; Tony wouldn't protect him. And he'd only tried to get close to Tony *after* failing to get close to any of the other partners. I don't know how he managed to last as long as he did.

I guess Muhammed was a practicing Muslim, but that was a surprise to me. I think his religion was a new development, if you know what I mean. He and I hung around together a few times before the Crash. Back in the city we went out for drinks a couple times on Friday after work. He had a huge stupid laugh and a big smile; great guy. Muhammed only drank whisky and he drank it straight because he said he didn't like beer. If we were out with other people, then he'd usually order appetizers and stuff for the whole table and he always ate the pork and the bacon and all of that. It was strange that he never really fit in at the firm, because he was a genuinely good fellow. Before the Crash, I never saw him pray like Muslims are supposed to pray. Anyway, I guess he returned to his faith right after that sonofabitch Randall told him that he would have to eat a bit of Givens or die. We each have different moral limits, and Muhammed's were well north of most everyone's out there, so he had flat refused to eat. Then, once he realized that they weren't waiting around for nature to take its course anymore, he decided to be proactive. So I've got mad respect for Muhammed because he chucked it all and said he'd rather die. He gathered up all the strength he had and walked out of the camp and didn't come back. He left a note. It was a short note and I remember it, even though I never saw it. I heard Jeffrey read it. It read:

"Today is my last day in this camp. Beginning tomorrow morning, I am walking out to look for rescue. I will have limited access to email but will be checking it frequently."

Kwame cried when he heard Muhammed's note, because Kwame felt that he was in danger.

We were down to that sonofabitch Randall, Carla, Tony Martin, Amy, Jeffrey, Kwame, and me. So Kwame was right to cry. He was next. The bit of Givens they'd eaten wasn't much between all of them and they were ready to hunt again. They'd already tried hunting me; they might have been desperate, but they weren't stupid enough to try me again. Kwame was in real danger.

Muhammed was a good guy who always tried to do the right thing. He had pretty much been a failure at the firm, though, and everyone knew it—or they should have known it. He just didn't fit in, wasn't willing to do what needed to be done. He tried to get by after the Crash, too, but I just don't think anyone wanted him around. And people like Muhammed can't cut it in a situation like that, because they can't lie to themselves. He was a good sort, but he had no hope of surviving out there alone.

I added Muhammed bin Muhammed to the *Catalog of the Dead.*

∞ ∞ ∞ ∞ ∞ ∞ ∞ ∞

ACT III: THE BEHEMOTH

The People Outside the Plane were so quiet for a day or so that I would have forgotten that they were out there except that Jeffrey checked on me every now and again just to "get a sense of the progress I was making". They sent Jeffrey to me with questions that no longer made sense. They asked me about the "radio repair" that I was doing because somehow they had got it in their heads that I was working on the plane's radio. I don't know anything about radios. But I played along.

"Working on it," I shouted out of the plane. I usually shouted out of the plane, very rarely left the plane anymore. "Doesn't look good. If I just had a sautering iron!" Yeah, that's what I said. It's actually a "soldering iron", but I didn't know that at the time. They didn't know that, either.

"Oh," they'd answer, then they'd grumble something about 'resource misallocation' and then limp back to the fire.

That sonofabitch Randall was still fat and in charge out there. He put Fire Team in charge of building commemorative pyres for each of the fallen attorneys. *His* pyre was the big, central fire around which they all sat all day and night and on which they would do their cooking. But around that he had them build one for each of us—even those of us who weren't dead, which should have been a warning to all of them, but they didn't pay close enough attention, I guess. He only let them light the pyres that were designated for those attorneys who had already fallen. But he was in charge, and he and Carla sent Jeffrey to the plane when they needed me to look for something, rather than coming over themselves. Maybe they were afraid of me. I usually don't think that they were afraid of me, but sometimes, looking back, I think that maybe they were a little afraid. It was smart of Randall and Carla to send Jeffery over, rather than coming over themselves—when you are running a calorie deficit like that, even walking thirty or forty feet is more work than you should do. That's how Carla lasted through to the next feast—she never came over to the plane, kept a low profile, and had Jeffrey do her research for her. Smart lady. Jeffrey's head got bigger and his ego swelled, because he was their go-to guy to come checking on me. I started to get tired of him because he checked on me all the time, like every three or four hours. I kept my distance from him because I was pretty certain that he wanted to kill me. He kept his distance from me, too.

∞ ∞ ∞ ∞ ∞ ∞ ∞ ∞

So about, I don't know, it must have been the 3rd or 4th day after Muhammed ran off to die alone and to not get eaten, Kwame woke up in the middle of the night and saw me sitting in the gash of the plane. His eyes opened wide because it had scared him to see me perched there like that. Kwame was probably the smartest guy in our group at the firm. He wouldn't have been at the firm for long even if the Crash hadn't happened—he would have left to be a professor or to become a judge or something. Guys like me, we get by, but Kwame was the real deal. He woke with a start, as if he'd been fighting to escape from a terrible dream. Also, he woke up because I tossed about a hundred pebbles over at him to wake him up.

"What are you doing?" he whispered.

"Nothing. Bring me those smokes over there," I said and pointed at the packet of cigarettes beside Jeffrey. Jeffrey and Amy were sleeping together by the fire.

Kwame grabbed the cigarettes and then walked over to me as best as he could. He was weak. I lit a cigarette for him and one for myself. Neither of us are smokers. But in times of desperation, you do desperate things. Plus, I was trying to make a deal with Kwame that could have saved us both, and I thought the gesture would help get the negotiation rolling.

"You're next," I said.

"What?"

"You're next. And they won't wait for nature."

"What?"

"You heard me," I said. "Billings was an asshole, but he wasn't a psychopath. Was Randall or Carla sent him after me. How long until they convince Jeffrey to come after you?"

"Are you sure that Billings was...trying...to kill you? Like, to eat you? Are you sure he wanted to kill you for food? That's crazy." Kwame believed me; he knew that I was right, but he couldn't bring himself to admit it that the People Outside the Plane had become so monstrous. Kwame protested because it was such a horrible thing to believe.

"Look around, Kwame," I said. "Look around. It's not safe for you. You can come in here with me—we can be safe in here. You and I always got along. So you can come in here. None of the others can come in here. Not even Tony."

"You and Tony are close," he said. "Don't you work with him...exclusively?"

"Jesus, Man. Tony's a decent sort, but they're all desperate. You can come in here now, but this is it. One time offer. After this, I don't know if I could trust you."

"I can't come in there," he said. "I can't. I can't live in there. It's too awful, Man. And when we get out of here...."

"If," I said.

"*If* we get out of here, I have to go back to work. I need two more years, Neal. Just two more years. Two more years and I can pay off my loans and get out. If I give up on Randall now—my career's over. You know that. I have to stick this out."

"You think? Giving up on Randall now...."

"Absolutely. And you know it," Kwame said. "If we get out of here and get back to the real world? Randall's all I've got right now. I can't pay my bills without this job, and I can't find another job without the firm's reference. I have to think about my future."

I thought about that for a while. Kwame was much smarter than me, and it bothered me to think that he was right. My career in biglaw was *already* ruined, probably. Probably. When I went in that plane—when I agreed to go into that plane—my career was probably over in the biglaw game. Eh.

"You're on your own out there," I said. "I'm not going to force you to do anything. Not going to make up your mind for you. But you're on your own out there. I'm sure you'll do what's right."

"What do we do?"

"We? What do you do, Man. Don't bring me out there. I offered to let you in the plane with me, but that's off the table now, Brother. So it's you and me, not we."

"You are *in* this with *us*," he said. "Come on, Man. Come on. Help me, Man. I can't come in there, but....What do I do?"

"I don't know," I said. "I am not saying you should do this or do that, I'm just telling you. Look at them." I motioned at Jeffrey and Amy who were sleeping together beside the fire. Kwame looked at the sleeping couple and exhaled a cloud of blue smoke from his lungs. "Jeffrey's a beast. He's a serious person. He and that sonofabitch Randall...."

"I work with Carla," Kwame interrupted me. "I'm protected. She's as bad as Randall. But she won't let anything bad happen to me."

I shook my head.

"You're as good as dead," I said. "In my opinion, you're as good as dead. Carla won't help you. Dead in the water. Unless we get rescued."

"We aren't getting rescued," Kwame said.

I nodded.

"You're a sonofabitch, Neal," Kwame said. "But you're right."

He smiled at me and we shook hands and then he went back to sleep beside the fire. He slept near Carla, but not all cuddled up. He was a smart guy, so I knew he'd do what he needed to do. I hoped it would be the *right* thing, but he was too smart for that.

He followed Amy down to the stream to gather water the next day and that's where he killed her. He claimed that she just fell over and died, but he killed her. He did it with his hands around her throat. I could tell that he did it this way because Amy didn't have any marks on her body, no stab wounds or anything. And her skull wasn't crush. And after he carried her body back from the stream, Kwame sat by the fire and couldn't stop looking at his hands. So I know that's how he did it: with his hands around her throat.

I added Amy to the *Catalog of the Dead*.

I can't blame Kwame for what he did. I would have done it if I were in his place, I think; I probably would have done it the same way, too. The People would have killed Kwame if he hadn't acted. They would have killed him at the first chance. Billings couldn't have done Kwame, because they were friends, but Billings was already dead. And Jeffrey? He could have done it. There was no love lost between Jeffrey and Kwame. They weren't even close. It wouldn't have been long before Amy got Jeffrey full on board with Carla and that sonofabitch Randall. I hate even thinking about this because, you know, I liked Tony a lot. I really did. But I need to just be honest and say that he was in on it, too, even if he didn't realize it. He was part of the team. So I should say that it wouldn't have been long before Amy got

Jeffrey full on board with Carla, *Tony*, and that sonofabitch Randall. Jeffrey would have killed Kwame, or Amy would have done it if Jeffrey didn't have the guts.

But Kwame killed both of them at once, really.

He, Tony, Carla, and that sonofabitch Randall ate Amy. Not all of her, but more than you would expect. They were famished. I hadn't seen it happen before, so I peaked out of the gash in the plane to see it with my own eyes. I could hear it happening, but I couldn't really *believe* it. I thought that, years later, I would look back and be completely unable to believe that I'd been so close to such pure evil. So I had to look, had to see it with my eyes so that I could always be certain. She was beside the fire all mangled and gnashed and she didn't look like a person anymore because they'd opened her up to get at her organs. Randall, that sonofabitch, used his knife to carve her up. The knife wasn't big enough for the job, so it was a bloody business and he had a hell of a time with the joints; he ended up using his hands to break the joints. They had parts of her roasting over the fire and it smelled like roasting pork tenderloin. It was disgusting. They'd given up carving joints after a debacle trying to carve her shoulder, so her hand was still full and human-looking on the roasting arm. Someone had taken her wedding ring. They hardly waited for her to cook and they hadn't bled her at all so there was blood on their faces and on their chins. They ate way too much because they were famished and then they each vomited. That fat tumor Randall must have eaten four pounds of her, fat and all. He was a disgusting man, all crouched on his haunches by the fire and slurping at the fat and gristle on the bone. They were so

69

wasteful—they roasted a leg, both arms, and a calf of the other leg, and they ate a few of the organs, but they tossed the rest away. It makes me feel sick even to think it, but, My God!, if you're going to do something so awful, at least do it 100% so you don't have to do it again. That sonofabitch Randall had an appetite without end, so they'd need more.

Jeffrey couldn't eat and he wouldn't sit near the fire, either. He was done for. He moved once, like he was moving toward the fire or maybe even for a last look at Amy's face, and Carla lashed out at him like an animal.

"Get the hell out of here!" she shouted. She swatted at him with the lit end of a stick. "Get back! You don't need to see this, you sonofabitch."

Jeffrey wasn't very likable. I didn't like him, at any rate. I never liked the way he smiled at me. He was cocksure and condescending, really full of himself, and just not at all that bright. No one really liked Jeffrey except for his crew of good old boys. The thing was, though, that he was a decent and good guy. He had a huge heart, too. That's why he broke down and cried so much. That's why he was so cocksure, too, because his heart was so big and he was only happy when he felt like he was in love with the world. Or when he felt like the world loved him, maybe.

Jeffrey went back to crying and doing that convulsing thing that he did when he cried. Kwame looked over the calf, or whatever it was he was eating, right at Jeffrey, and he stared at Jeffrey while he ate. Kwame was a smart guy. When I had woken him up that night, I thought for sure he'd take Jeffrey while he slept. But Kwame got Jeffrey and Amy at the same time, really, because Jeffrey was broken completely now. Jeffrey didn't have Amy propping him up anymore, and he had lost Randall's respect, too, because he hadn't been able to do what needed to be done with me. He was a good guy in his own way, even though he was probably trying to kill me so that everyone could eat my corpse. So Kwame was in the golden seat there for a bit. The only question, really, was whether he would wait for Jeffrey to die on his own or whether they would kill Jeffrey. And Jeffrey wouldn't run, not like Muhammed had run.

I watched them all eat and I swear that Kwame winked at me, like maybe he was signaling that "everything was cool" between him and me. Like maybe he was saying that he wanted me to be safe, too, just like he was, and that all we would have to do now was wait and then out last fat old Randall and Carla. And, damnit, Tony.

∞ ∞ ∞ ∞ ∞ ∞ ∞

Jeffrey lasted about a week, I'd say. We'd lost track of time. I got to see this one.

It was the middle of the day and I was sitting in the gash on the plane. The People Outside the Plane were sitting around the central fire and not talking with one another. They were just sitting. That sonofabitch Randall and Carla kept looking at each other, though. Little glances, you couldn't miss them. Even though their faces had grown gaunt (although Randall still had the paunchy neck) and their eyes were starting to sink in and look hollow, you still couldn't mistake it: They were communicating. It was really something to watch, like an

71

anthropological study. I don't know. I enjoyed watching it, from a purely anthropological standpoint, obviously. Under normal circumstances, I wouldn't by choice watch a couple of people plot to kill a third person. But in desperate times, you take solace in desperate entertainment, I suppose. Randall and Carla nodded at each other and then Carla slid over closer to Kwame.

She nodded at Kwame.

Then Kwame stood up and walked around the fire and stood behind Jeffrey. Jeffrey *knew* what was going on, but he was too weak and scared and confused to do anything about it. He just said, "Even me?" Kwame had a rock in his hand and I wondered if I'd have the stomach to watch him do it. I did.

He did it.

I added Jeffrey to the *Catalog of the Dead*.

They ate Jeffrey for two days and then carried what was left of his body off into the woods for the wolves and the bears and what not. Deep into the night, I could sometimes hear rustling out along the edges of the camp from the animals that had learned of our camp. There would be nothing left of Barnes or Muhammed, obviously, but also nothing left of Givens, nothing left of Amy or Jeffrey. Wolves would even dig up the makeshift graves of Elwes and Denny Simons, using their snouts and paws to move away the stones to get at their corpses. Nothing would be left out there of the dead.

Kwame slept easy after that because he felt that he was safe. He didn't think he had any competition left because, after all, the partners were all on his side now with him doing their dirty work. The remaining question was whether he and Randall would kill

Tony next, or Carla. Sometimes I thought there was a chance that Kwame might "manage up" and get Carla and Tony to kill Randall. I'm serious, Kwame was the most talented person I've ever met. If he'd had *real* ambition, he could have been anything he wanted to be at the firm. Hell, a guy like that could have *been the firm*—but he just didn't have that kind of ambition. He was a good guy, I think, despite everything that happened.

∞ ∞ ∞ ∞ ∞ ∞

I stayed in the airplane a lot over the next week or so. So I don't know how it happened, but I bet it was a hell of row when they killed Carla because Carla was the fiercest woman who I've ever known. She was strong and she was mean. And she would have put up a hell of a fight so that it probably took more than one of them, at least two of them, acting in concert to kill her.

But then one day I stopped hearing Carla's voice.

I added Carla to the *Catalog of the Dead.*

When I poked my head out of the plane, there were Kwame and Randall feasting. Disgusting. Yes, Tony was there, too. I worked for Tony so much, worked *with* Tony so much. He taught me how to be an attorney. He wasn't like a father to me, so don't get that idea, but he was a *mentor.* He taught me everything that you'd think they'd teach you in law school, but don't. Tony would take time to slow down, to teach, to discuss, to make sure I *really* understood. He did that at great personal cost to himself sometimes, too—helping me through things in late night phone calls, coming into the office on a Friday night or a Saturday to help with motions or sections of briefs. If it hadn't been for the Crash, I probably would have made partner one day; if that had happened, I think I would have pulled Tony aside and said, "you know, I wouldn't have made it if it hadn't been for your help." But there's no use thinking about that kind of nonsense now; the Crash destroyed all of those dreams, didn't it? It was difficult for me to see Tony eating like that, because I didn't want to see him all inhuman and ravenous. I didn't want to believe that I had been wrong about him.

And Tony didn't kill Kwame, but he was complicit in it. I can accept it now that Tony knew the plan all along. God that's a heartbreaker. Kwame didn't see it coming. He must have thought he'd be safe for at least as long as they were eating on Carla's corpse. But he was wrong. He underestimated Randall, and that was a mistake that would cost him his life.

That sonofabitch Randall knew that he couldn't compete with Kwame after they'd both eaten. Kwame was young and strong and he was smart as hell—it was his youth that was dangerous, I think, because Kwame didn't need to sleep, he could be calm and cool under pressure even without sleep, and he didn't *need* to eat like Randall. He could do with less, and that's a dangerous thing in a situation like we were in where food is all that matters. That sonofabitch Randall got him by surprise.

Randall met eyes with me while he was eating part of Carla. He was grotesque, Man. Greasy, fat with meat, hands swollen and strong. His knife lay across his lap and the cudgel rested at his side. It dawned on me that the knife looked a lot like the knife I had given to Justine when she walked out, but that thought was too awful to consider, so I pushed it out of my mind. He looked right at me and I swear to you that he smiled. Then he put down the hank of meat he was working on, wiped his hands on his navy blue suit pants, grabbed his knife, and killed Kwame while he ate. Kwame was smiling and eating and having a grand old time when Randall poked him in the throat and then a couple of times in the chest. Kwame died quickly and died with a smile on his face, though, so I guess that's good? It's the best he could have hoped for, I suppose.

That sonofabitch Randall even looked at me through the gash in the plane right after he killed Kwame. He didn't smile at me, but it looked like he wanted to. He knew that I was watching and he'd killed Kwame because he wanted me to see it happen. They didn't need the meat. Carla could have kept them going for a couple of weeks, anyway. He did it because he knew that, in the end, it would be him or me and he wanted me to know that he was capable of vast evil.

I cried a bit when I added Kwame to the *Catalog of the Dead*. We were friends.

∞ ∞ ∞ ∞

That sonofabitch Randall had a heyday out there. I could hear him guffawing, laughing. He was even singing! I'm not even kidding. He had a big awful baritone voice and he belted out that *Bye Bye Baby* song. He'd probably heard me humming it or singing it. It was the last song I'd heard during the Crash and it had been stuck in my head ever since. Sometimes I sing when I work and I don't even recognize that I'm doing it. I must have put the song in his head while I was working on the *Catalog of the Dead.* He was having a grand time out there, though, now that he had more than enough to eat.

But Tony.

I don't know what happened to Tony. It doesn't matter how old you are, there's real heartbreak when your mentors let you down. When someone who you respect and who you look up to fails you—and they will fail you—it's just like being a kid again when your favorite team doesn't win. It was just heartbreaking to see Tony out there acting like a lap dog, feasting with Randall and laughing at Randall's stupid jokes. It was just the two of them now, and Tony went on smiling and laughing as though the two of them could go on like that forever in a bizarre and morbid re-telling of the Odd Couple. The theme to that old show went through my mind. Do da do da doooo...do da dooo, do da doooo do.

It was because of Tony that I barricaded myself into the plane. No one believes this when I tell them; everyone thinks I did it because I was scared. Maybe I was scared a little. Ok, yes, I was scared. I was more scared than I'd ever been. Every day I was out there, my life was a nightmare; I lived in fear and in fright; yes, yes, ok. Ok. I admit that. But I barricaded myself in because I couldn't stand to watch Tony, who I respected, acting like such a fool. Laughing, eating and telling jokes, and thinking that somehow *he* was different. Thinking that *he* was the one who Randall really loved. Randall, that was nothing more than a beast. To see Tony believe that....

I couldn't watch. Couldn't believe it was reality. I tried to tell myself that it was all an act.

And I was torn.

If it was an act, then Tony was little more than a monster waiting for his chance to become as fat with meat as Randall; waiting for the right moment to set upon his master and slay him, just as Randall had killed all of us one by one. Even if Tony was acting a part out there, he was doing it because he wanted to survive in a gruesome game.

On the other hand, if it wasn't an act...if he was *drinking the Kool Aid,* or whatever you want to call it...then he must have been looking for a way to offer me up to Randall. I was the only one left. In my mind, Tony could only be waiting to kill Randall or waiting to kill me. I could not see any other play for him.

So I barricaded myself into the plane, because I couldn't stand to watch my mentor behave that way. There were hundreds of seats and seat frames. I'd ripped into the wall of the plane and yanked out hundreds and hundreds of feet of wiring and there were even a few lengths of rope on the plane. So I had all I needed. I used the seat frames to make a barricade and I fastened it tight with rope and with long lengths of steel and bones from the dead. I didn't want to know what would happen out there, and I didn't want them coming in the plane. I'd stockpiled enough wood and water for several weeks or a month, if I were frugal.

Now, just to be honest here, until that point, I'd understood everything that happened. I didn't agree with everyone's decisions, of course, but I could understand them. Obviously I could relate to Muhammed's and to Justine's decisions, but I have to admit that I could *also* relate to Jeffrey, to Kwame, even to

Amy and even, even, even to Randall, that sonofabitch. But what happened next made no sense to me. The mind boggles at the strength of human commitment. After several days of their feasting and singing and dancing, I heard that sonofabitch Randall shouting:

"NEAL! NEAL! NEAL!"

I stood and looked through one of the broken out windows of the fuselage and there were Randall and Tony. There was still meat left on Kwame, still meat on Carla. But Tony was on his knees kneeling with his back to Randall. Randall had the cudgel in his hand. He yelled "NEAL!" again and then he saw me looking out the porthole at him. He smiled.

"Go ahead and say it," he said to Tony. And Tony said, haltingly but half-shouting so that I could hear it:

"Our Father, Who art in Heaven, hallowed be Thy Name. Thy Kingdom come, Thy Will be done on Earth as it is in Heaven. Give us this day our daily bread and forgive us our trespasses as we forgive those who trespass against us. Lead us not into temptation, but deliver us from evil. Amen."

Then Randall killed Tony with the cudgel to the back of his head. It was one blow while he knelt, then a pause for Randall to stare me down. Then he fell upon the corpse and crushed the skull from behind with two more blows.

I bawled like a scared child when I added Tony to the *Catalog of the Dead*.

I felt very alone and vulnerable. And I was in great danger.

∞ ∞ ∞

Then it was just that sonofabitch Randall and me. You've never seen anything like it—he was a monster. I wasn't scared or even intimidated because I'd given up all hope of rescue and I wasn't afraid of dying anymore. I'm not sure I've ever been afraid of dying; maybe that's why I was such a failure at the firm— Muhammed and the others failed, but they each had different reasons, their own reasons, for why they did the things that they did. But I think that if you look closely at a Great Man, in any field really, but especially at a big law firm, you'll find someone who is deeply afraid of death. So I didn't fear Randall, but I respected him.

I used the dead bodies in the plane to strengthen the barricade over the gash in the plane. Randall couldn't get in, but I couldn't get out, either. The plane was dark and lonely as hell for a long, long time. I didn't even leave the plane to piss, I just did it in the bathroom until the tank was full and then in the dark corner of the cockpit. I slept near the gash in the plane where fresh air would sometimes come in through the cracks between the seats that I used to block the gash and where I could keep my ears and eyes open for that sonofabitch Randall. It got cold, too, and the days were short. He built thirteen smaller fires in a ring around his big central pyre, too, so that the firelight made it bright outside like an arena at night. He shouted loudly the whole time, explaining *everything* he was doing—that each fire commemorated one of our fallen, and so he lit only twelve. That fat tumor of a man out there kept his fires raging at all hours; he built his central pyre so large that I could hear it, the snapping and popping of the wood, sometimes the hiss or whoosh of a jet of heat escaping the bottom of the fire where the coals glowed. I could hear their fat pop and sizzle when he roasted bits of them. He cooked what was left of Carla and Kwame and he smoked a lot of Tony's meat over the huge fire, and then he ate on them until the meat began to turn. It took weeks. I peaked out the windows during the days to monitor how much food he had. He ate too quickly, gorging himself. Most days he would get into a frenzy and eat and eat until he was so full that he had to purge and then he'd vomit in the woods, return to eating. He cracked open the bones with rocks, fingered out the marrow and lapped it off of his swollen fingers.

I still had the stone that Billings had killed himself on. To kill the time, I took the length of metal from a seat frame that was a type of blunt spear and I used the stone to sharpen the end of it into a real spear.

His appetite was too large, too demanding. Randall wasn't even a man anymore—he was something else. A monster. He grew weak when he couldn't eat and then at the first chance he feasted like a mad, ancient behemoth become carnivore. He raged and snarled at his food as he ate and at the Earth when he walked and at every living creature unless he knew that he had them or wanted them, and then he would smile that broad tight smile that sent his fat cheeks up to his eyes. At night he stalked around the raging fire with ponderous footsteps that shook the ground and rattled the pines; he roared in the night so fierce and so powerfully that it shook my lungs and woke me from nightmares.

"Come on out here! The night is beautiful and I've got a project for you!"

I would not budge. I stayed resolute inside while the maniac laughed outside, while he made me promises of food and freedom and rescue. Sometimes I paced, sometimes I sat cross-legged for hours. Sometimes I slept, one eye open. Waiting.

He'd stare at the plane while he ate, scanning the plane to find me. Usually he couldn't find me, but sometimes he'd see me peering out one of the windows and we'd lock eyes. He stared at me, smiling as he chewed. He ate so much so fast; it must have been painful for him. His gut swelled sometimes and after a big feast he'd have to unbutton his wragged dress pants and lean back, belching and licking his fingers. There was no logic in how much or how fast that he ate—he must have been eating that much *to prevent me from eating* his store of meat. He was primordial. But I don't think he understood me or the situation. I didn't want to eat Kwame or Carla. I didn't want to eat Tony. I swear: I never ate a bit of it, never even a bite of it. So he was just wasting his food reserve in his game to better me. I laid low and waited for him to eat himself into a corner.

Then what was left of the meat turned and he was without again.

At first he was angry and frustrated when the meat ran out. I could hear him shouting out there. He shouted at me:

"NEAL! Was it the altimeter, do you think? JESUS CHRIST WHAT HAPPENED? WHAT WERE THE PILOTS THINKING!"

I cowered lower, waiting.

"Radar," he moaned. "Radar. Don't they have RADAR?"

In his frustration he also shouted at Kwame and at Carla, even Kent and Simons. "Goddamn it, Kent—don't you have a pilot's license? What the HELL good is a pilot's license if you can't pilot a plane? If you were worth a goddamn, you would have gone into that cockpit and stopped this!" He shouted, "Carla you fucking bitch, I loved you but you really let me down here. Bitch!" They were all dead and bits of some of them were in his belly but he shouted at them. He blamed them for his situation and he cursed and shouted at Kwame because his meat had turned faster than Carla's. In his rage and madness he finally settled in on me and was determined to fight his way into the plane to get at me or to get at the corpses that I had protected from his hunger. He pounded against the wall of the fuselage and gnashed and pummeled against my barricade over the gash in the fuselage. I set myself strong against the inside of the barricade of seat frames, rope, and bone, and pushed back against it with everything I had. I am not a strong man, but I'd woven the seat frames together well and had lashed them tightly down, blocking them together with the bones of the dead. He couldn't get through. Sometimes I saw an eye of the beast leering in between the cracks of the seat backs and chair frames, and sometimes his fat finger or a whole hand would burst through one of the large cracks and grasp for me. But he could not have me.

I waited there indefinitely among the dead.

I almost gave in at times, chucked it.

A couple of weeks after Tony was gone, that sonofabitch Randall's shouting and huffing slowed. His rages grew infrequent and his voice sounded weaker. Now that all his food was gone he started limping again. His injuries from the Crash hadn't actually healed, but had only grown less pronounced when he was well fed. He moved less and spent long hours sitting beside his raging pyre inside his ring of signal fires.

I began taking down the barricade. It took a while because I'd built it up and reinforced it a couple of times. When I got it open, it was a clear and crisp day at the very end of winter, or maybe even into the spring, and he was sprawled out beside the fire.

"There you are you sonofabitch," he said to me. He had a huge smile on his face. "I knew you'd come around! I always knew you were the best one on the team! Get over here. I've got a project for you."

"Do you?" I asked as I stepped out of the plane. "I'm kind of busy, but I'll see what I can do. What do you need?"

"What are you working on these days?" he asked me.

"The *Catalog of the Dead*," I answered. I tapped at my chest pocket with the point of the spear, where I carried the notebook and kept track of the dead.

"Jesus, Neal. What the hell have you even been doing in there? The *Catalog*? That old thing? This whole time? You're not done with that yet?"

"Not yet," I told him. "But I'll have it by the end of the day."

∞ ∞

I was three weeks out there alone. That was nice. To tell you the truth, I'd always had a fantasy about surviving a plane crash all alone in the middle of nowhere. Or maybe with just one other person or two other people. That sonofabitch Randall had 8 months' worth of firewood stored up beside the camp. He'd had them working in shifts to collect it, I think. The stream was clear and nice, but it was too cold for fish. I used tarpaulin from the plane to pitch a little tent beside the fire and I scrounged some metal off the outside of the plane to ring half the fire so that all the heat came back to me and I had all the blankets I could wish for; I stayed warm through the cold nights.

It was a biologist who finally found me. His name is Ricky. Ricky studies birds for a living. Really happy guy; birds are his life. It's almost all he can think about or talk about. Seemed like a nice guy, but he was surprised as hell to see me. He'd heard about the Crash and he told me that everyone had stopped looking for us months earlier. Ricky would hardly speak to me at first because he was shocked to have found me and he was frightened of me, I think. Wouldn't you be? It's scary to run into someone in the middle of nowhere when you think you're all alone in the world. He told me that the authorities had given up searching because "no one knew where we were"—I didn't comment at the time, but that reasoning made no sense. Obviously no one knew where we were, and that's a damn fine reason *not* to give up searching. I asked him if the firm had hired any special extra help to search but he didn't know; he didn't know anything about lawyers or law firms. The only thing he knew about that was that, once the word got out that there were so many attorneys on the flight, there were jokes floating around about how the crash might have been for the best. "What do you call an airplane lost in the mountains with 15 attorneys aboard? A good start." I didn't think that was funny because we were real people.

The authorities had searched for us for weeks but they could not see us from the sky, and Ricky understood why no one had found us when he saw how we were wedged into the canyon. Apparently we were way off course for some reason, too. I don't know why. It could have been the radar or the altimeter or pilot error, I don't know. I don't care why. The black box transmitter thing hadn't worked, so even after they found the plane there was no way to know what went wrong—first time in history that a black box failed like that, or at least the first time that the company that makes black boxes would admit to. There is a lawsuit against the airline ongoing, and I guess damages will depend a little on who survived the crash and on how long they survived, and then the families of the dead will get money. That's why they need my story. I guess. I don't get any money because I lived. That doesn't seem fair to me, but that's the law, I guess. An attorney for the airline told me that was the law and I just haven't gotten around to looking into it. He could be lying to me.

"Are you OK?" Ricky asked me.

"Yeah, I'm ok. I've been better."

"What happened out here?" he asked. He was nervous. He wouldn't come close to me at first, and he was crouched low the closer he got to me like he was protecting himself and getting ready to run at the slightest reason. I wasn't going to hurt him, though.

"Long story," I said. "Four kids left to get out. I guess they didn't make it. And a woman. Justine Moore. Have you heard of Justine Moore? Has anyone heard from her yet?"

"This canyon is damn near inaccessible," the biologist said. I was in fine form, really. I invited him over and we sat together by the fire. "Three seasons ago there was a ptarmigan nest back near the back of this canyon that I watched. Was just coming to check on it."

"I haven't seen any birds," I said. "I was in the plane for a long time. Don't go in the plane."

"What's in there?"

"Bodies," I said. "A lot of bodies. I've got a list of the names. There were about 150 people on the plane. Four walked out. Or maybe six walked out. Technically, seven, but one of them is dead for sure. The rest are dead."

"Can you walk?" he asked me.

"I could walk out of here if I knew what direction to walk in. I just haven't left because I don't know where to go. I thought Justine Moore might come back for me. Have you seen her?"

"I haven't seen her, Man," Ricky said. He scooted closer to me, but was still nervous so he had his hand up like to calm me down. "But we'll find her when we get you out of here."

"She might be alive," I said.

"Maybe," Ricky said. He didn't believe me. "There's a lot of great campground around here. Maybe she stopped down canyon and is waiting out the winter. There's a God's plenty to eat and drink just down that way."

"Yeah," I said. "I bet she did. She's probably got an artist's colony going down there. Or a bed and breakfast near the sea. Maybe she opened a restaurant. Nothing fancy, of course, but classy, you know. Real tablecloths and earthy comfort food. Or she could be writing, too, I guess. Her novel."

"Ok, buddy," he said. "Ok. I'm gonna get you out of here."

"Ok, Ok," I said. "I get it. Well...how far a walk out is it?"

"Four days," he said. "If you go the right direction and make good time. Can you walk? Are you hungry?"

"No, I'm good," I said. "I'll just grab a bottle of water from the stream down there and we can head out."

"What have you been eating?" he asked me. He knew. It was pretty clear for anyone with eyes to see what had happened.

"I didn't do that," I said. "I didn't eat any of that. They all did, many of them. I wouldn't do it."

"What happened?"

I couldn't talk about it just then.

People want to hear about it, the cannibalism; they want to hear it and then to wonder whether they'd do the same in the same situation. Some people cringe when I tell the story and I know that they hate all my former colleagues, think they were evil and that what they did after the Crash was just in their evil nature. A lot of people say that we got what was coming to us—we knew the risks when we got on the plane. Some people are more understanding, though, and they say, "My God. May God have mercy on their souls." One way or another, though, everyone judges them. No one stays impartial. Anyone who hears it either indicts or absolves in their mind all those lawyers from what they did out there.

I don't blame any of us who were stuck out there after the Crash, I don't think. They were all good people. It's as simple as that. They were good people, but the situation was pretty rough. After the Crash they had to do what they had to do out there outside the plane. You eat what you kill out there, Man. Unless you got a bunch of peanuts and potato chips. There was like two years' worth of food and water on that plane, if I were frugal.

It was a beautiful hike out, though difficult. We hiked without a trail the first day, scraping along the side of a mountain in the pine forest. There were blazes on the trees that I think Ricky had put there for his own good, because I got the feeling that Ricky was about the only guy who ever spent any time on that mountainside. Ricky was patient with me and I did a good job keeping up with him, given the ordeal I'd been through. Sometimes when I started to think about the crash and everything that had happened I would get weak or jittery and Ricky would have to carry me, or at least help me along. He was very patient. I had never seen anything like that mountainside. Just gorgeous. We climbed up and down the side of the mountain for a day and then we camped on a crest over a clear brook—maybe even the same one from the canyon, but I can't say because I was lost. Then the next day was hard hiking again, but Ricky knew his way around and I was feeling pretty strong because Ricky had plenty of freeze dried food that he kept making and feeding to me. He was quite an outdoorsman and he knew the lay of the forest well. We were another day without a trail, but it wasn't difficult hiking that day; the ground was level enough, there was no scree, and there was very little undergrowth to fight through on that last day. We found a set of switchbacks on the last day of the hike and followed those down to a logging road. We had to hike another several miles to find Ricky's truck where he'd parked it alongside the gravel road. He talked the whole way about how excited my family would be when they heard that I was alive, but I told him that I didn't have any family and he got quiet. Then he said, "Well, your friends then", but then I told him that I didn't really have any friends anymore, either, because since I'd joined the firm my only friends were attorneys in my group and they were all dead and that my fiancée had left me shortly before the Crash. She said I was too much of a dreamer and that I was always depressed and in a bad mood and she just didn't want to deal with that. I couldn't blame her, I told Ricky, because I had been in a pretty bad mood for most of my life. Ricky started walking a little faster when we could see his truck, just about a quarter of a mile away down the road. He tossed his pack into the back of the truck and we got into the truck and he started the thing and turned on the radio. It was the first time I'd heard a radio in weeks and it killed me that there was a radio station that came in up there because I thought that meant that if we'd just had a working radio and maintained contact then none of it would have happened. We were about to go but then he said, "Oh, hey, look at that!"

He jogged over to the other side of the road and picked something up. I got out to walk around the truck and a guy on the radio said "Your home of classic hits of the 70s, that's right!

Next up, the Bay City Rollers and their Four Seasons classic...."
Coincidences, Man. That's all that is. Ricky held up something
that he'd found on the side of the road so that I could see it; I'd
come around the front of the truck.

"It's an iPhone!" he said. "Imagine that! All the way up here
and someone lost their phone!" He pulled it from the plastic sack
and handed the sack to me as he tried to turn it on. The battery
was dead. Justine Moore had made it at least as far as that road.
The notebook I'd given to her was in the Ziploc bag, too. I was
not thinking straight. I slid the notebook out and flipped it open,
starting from the last page, hoping that she would have written
down everything—where she was, where she had been, what
she'd been through and how she'd made it out. But all the pages
were empty except the first one. The first page of the notebook
read: "The forest is so big." I couldn't breathe for a minute and I
had pressure in my chest and then I went mad.

I ran down the road, screaming "Justine! Justine!" and running
and screaming. I was bawling. Bawling as heavy as Jeffrey had
when we crashed and he'd lost it. Then I bounded off the road
and into the trees, running and screaming. "JUSTINE!
JUSTINE!" Ricky couldn't keep up with me. Screaming and
running and crying. I ran through the forest at random, screaming
all the time although I couldn't hear myself screaming for my
heartbeat and for how loud my pulse was against my eardrums,
and looking everywhere I could behind trees and beside fallen
logs for any sign of her or of which way she might have gone, and
then I would bound back up onto the road and run along it,
screaming "Justine!". Now that I was down there off the

mountainside I started to understand why we hadn't been found, why we were so lost up there.

I fell to my knees in the middle of the road and shouted, "JUSTINE!" It echoed against the canyon above us, through the trees, and the whole forest resonated with my awful crying. "JUSTINE! JUSTINE!" Ricky tried to calm me, but I fought him off, stood and ran again. "JUSTINE!" I was back off the road and into the trees, screaming.

I understood then the enormity of the forest and the enormity of my own evil.

I ran until I collapsed and lost consciousness.

Sometimes I wake up in the middle of the night thinking that she might be out there somewhere, living and breathing the same air that I am, maybe even close by, like we might just be missing each other by a few moments every day at the supermarket. I dream most nights that I find her and that she forgives me for everything, as if she has that power. Sometimes I think that she might have made it, run out through the forest, and then started her life all over and did it all right this time and not made the same mistakes a second time. I know it doesn't make sense to believe that she could be, that she could have made it out through that ordeal.

It's difficult to hope.

But it's possible.

People are amazing.

About the Author

Tyler Coulson was born in rural Illinois. He graduated with distinction from the University of Iowa College of Law and practiced in the corporate reorganization group of a leading international firm in Chicago. In 2011, he walked across the United States with his dog, Mabel. He lives in Chicago.

Other Titles

Check out these other great titles by Tyler Coulson:

BY MEN OR BY THE EARTH. The incredible story of Coulson's 2011 cross-country walk. It is the story of how and why he set out to walk across North America and of what he learned along the way. Part memoir, part revelation, part self-criticism, part instruction manual—Coulson's account is an honest, sometimes brutally honest, depiction of a flawed man struggling to survive in a flawed system, and of the unshakeable bond between a man and his dog.

THE ASSOCIATE OF STRATFORD-UPON-AVON. To be, or not to be? That is the question...presented in a legal memo that will change the life of young William Shakespeare. The greatest writer in the history of the English language is recast as a struggling young barrister in this inventive and poignant comedy. Shakespeare and his moody law partner, Charles Ap Ulet, gamble their failing law practice on a single client, Prince Hamlet of Denmark, and his claim of "wrongful death" against his uncle, King Claudius. Shakespeare has no experience, no evidence, and no idea where the courthouse is. But with luck, he might change the course of legal history.